NANCY DREW
girl detective®

PAPERCUTZ™

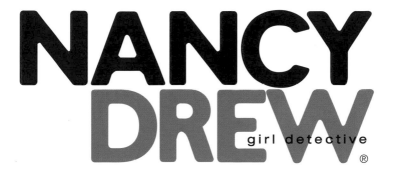

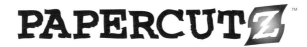

NANCY DREW
girl detective®

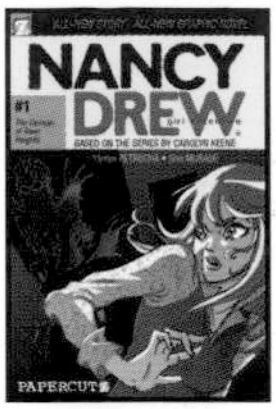
NANCY
DREW
PAPERCUT

Graphic Novels
Available from Papercutz

#1 The Demon of River Heights
#2 Writ In Stone
#3 The Haunted Dollhouse
#4 The Girl Who Wasn't There
#5 The Fake Heir
#6 Mr. Cheeters Is Missing (coming August 2006)

$7.95 each in paperback
$12.95 each in hardcover

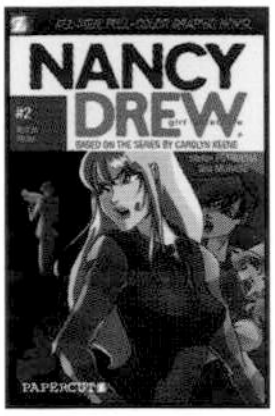
NANCY
DREW
PAPERCUT

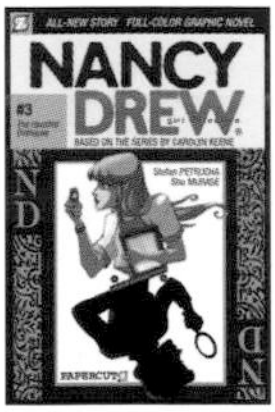
NANCY
DREW
PAPERCUT

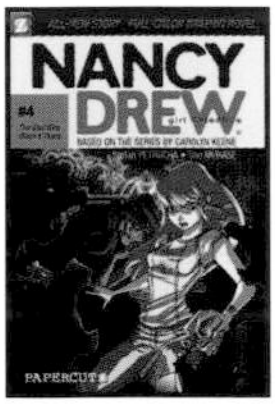
NANCY
DREW
PAPERCUT

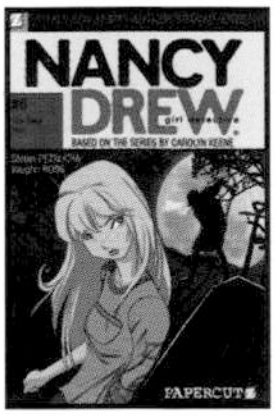
NANCY
DREW
PAPERCUT

Please add $3.00 for postage and handling for the first book, add $1.00 for each additional book.

Send for our catalog:
Papercutz
555 Eighth Avenue, Suite 1202
New York, NY 10018
www.papercutz.com

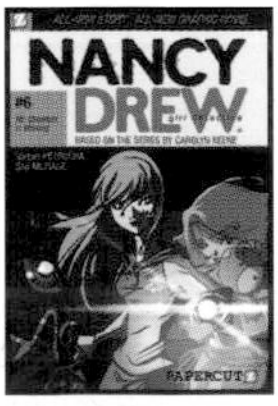
NANCY
DREW
PAPERCUT

NANCY DREW
#5 DREW
girl detective ®

The Fake Heir

STEFAN PETRUCHA • Writer
DANIEL VAUGHN ROSS • Artist
with 3D CG elements by LUIS LUNDGREN
Cover, preview pages, and art direction by SHO MURASE
Based on the series by
CAROLYN KEENE

PAPERCUTZ ™
New York

The Fake Heir
STEFAN PETRUCHA – Writer
DANIEL VAUGHN ROSS – Artist
with 3D CG elements by LUIS LUNDGREN
BRYAN SENKA – Letterer
CARLOS JOSE GUZMAN – Colorist
JIM SALICRUP
Editor-in-Chief

project sunshine
bringing sunshine to a cloudy day℠

Nancy Drew volunteers with Project Sunshine.
Project Sunshine is a nonprofit organization that provides free
services to children and families affected by medical challenges.
We send volunteers to hospitals to provide arts and crafts, tutoring
and other special services. For more information on Project
Sunshine please visit www.projectsunshine.org.

ISBN 10: 1-59707-024-6 paperback edition
ISBN 13: 978-1-59707-024-9 paperback edition
ISBN 10: 1-59707-025-4 hardcover edition
ISBN 13: 978-1-59707-025-6 hardcover edition

Printed in China.
Distributed by Holtzbrinck Publishers.

10   9   8   7   6   5   4   3   2   1

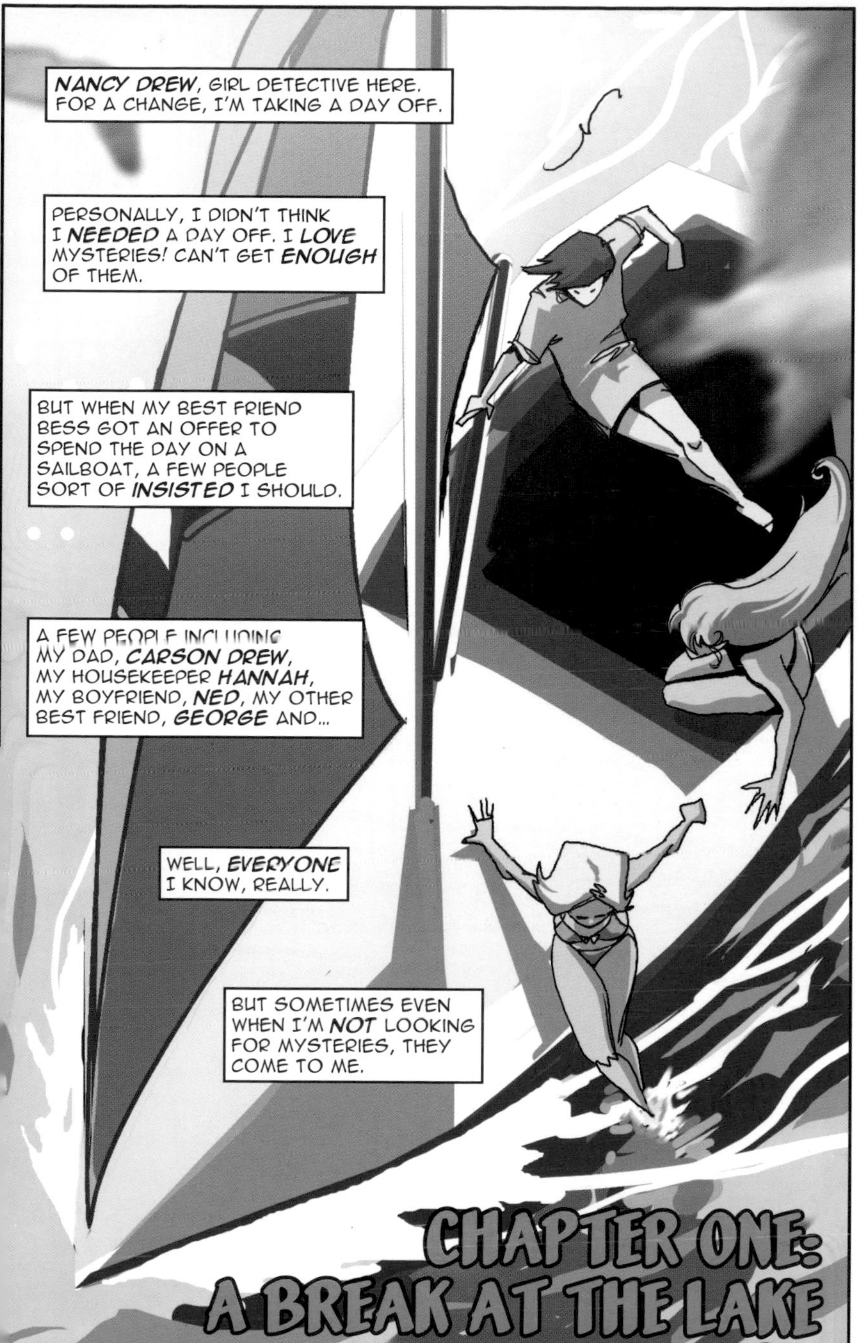
NANCY DREW, GIRL DETECTIVE HERE. FOR A CHANGE, I'M TAKING A DAY OFF.
PERSONALLY, I DIDN'T THINK I NEEDED A DAY OFF. I LOVE MYSTERIES! CAN'T GET ENOUGH OF THEM.
BUT WHEN MY BEST FRIEND BESS GOT AN OFFER TO SPEND THE DAY ON A SAILBOAT, A FEW PEOPLE SORT OF INSISTED I SHOULD.
A FEW PEOPLE INCLUDING MY DAD, CARSON DREW, MY HOUSEKEEPER HANNAH, MY BOYFRIEND, NED, MY OTHER BEST FRIEND, GEORGE AND...
WELL, EVERYONE I KNOW, REALLY.
BUT SOMETIMES EVEN WHEN I'M NOT LOOKING FOR MYSTERIES, THEY COME TO ME.
CHAPTER ONE: A BREAK AT THE LAKE

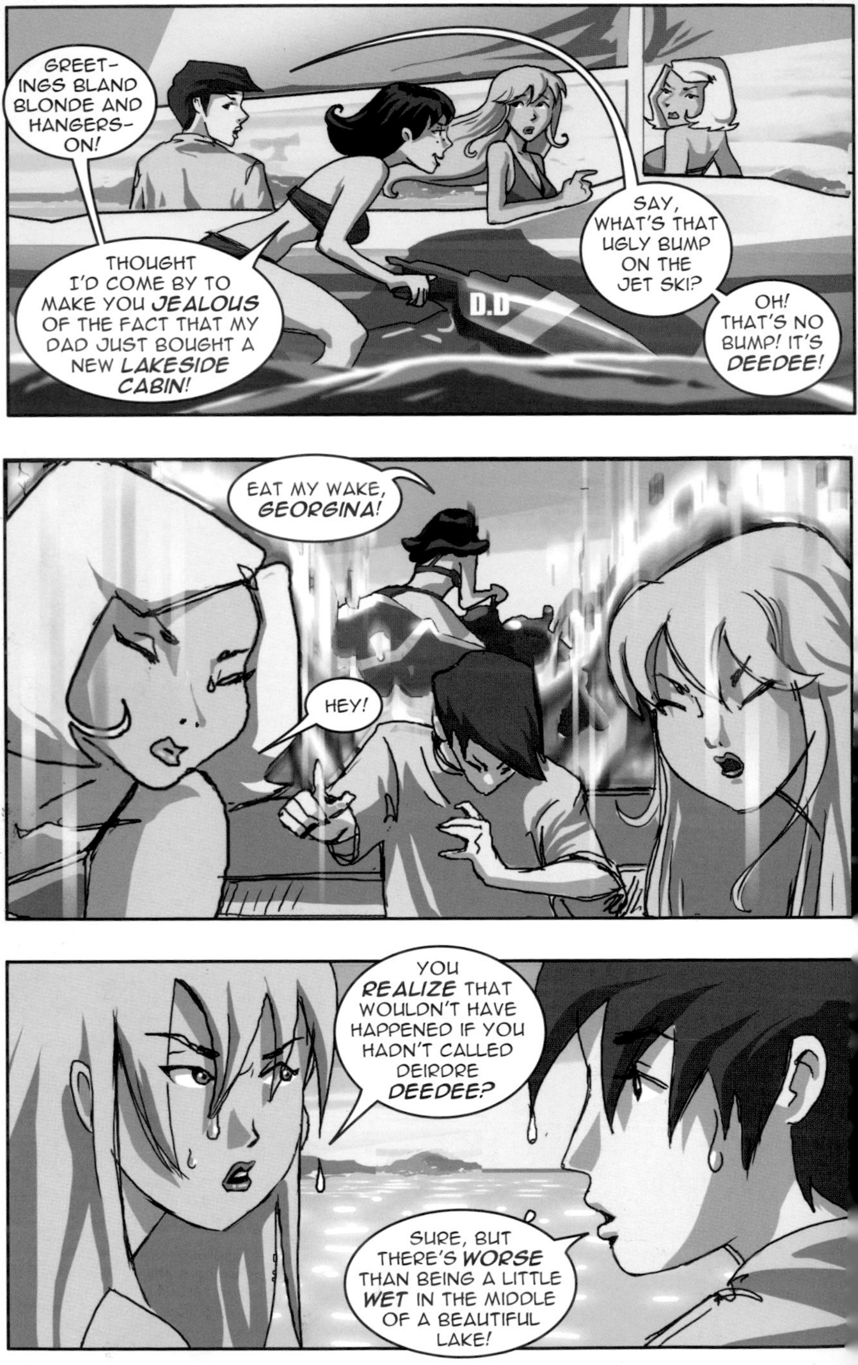
GREETINGS BLAND BLONDE AND HANGERS-ON!
THOUGHT I'D COME BY TO MAKE YOU JEALOUS OF THE FACT THAT MY DAD JUST BOUGHT A NEW LAKESIDE CABIN!
SAY, WHAT'S THAT UGLY BUMP ON THE JET SKI?
OH! THAT'S NO BUMP! IT'S DEEDEE!
D.D
EAT MY WAKE, GEORGINA!
HEY!
YOU REALIZE THAT WOULDN'T HAVE HAPPENED IF YOU HADN'T CALLED DEIRDRE DEEDEE?
SURE, BUT THERE'S WORSE THAN BEING A LITTLE WET IN THE MIDDLE OF A BEAUTIFUL LAKE!

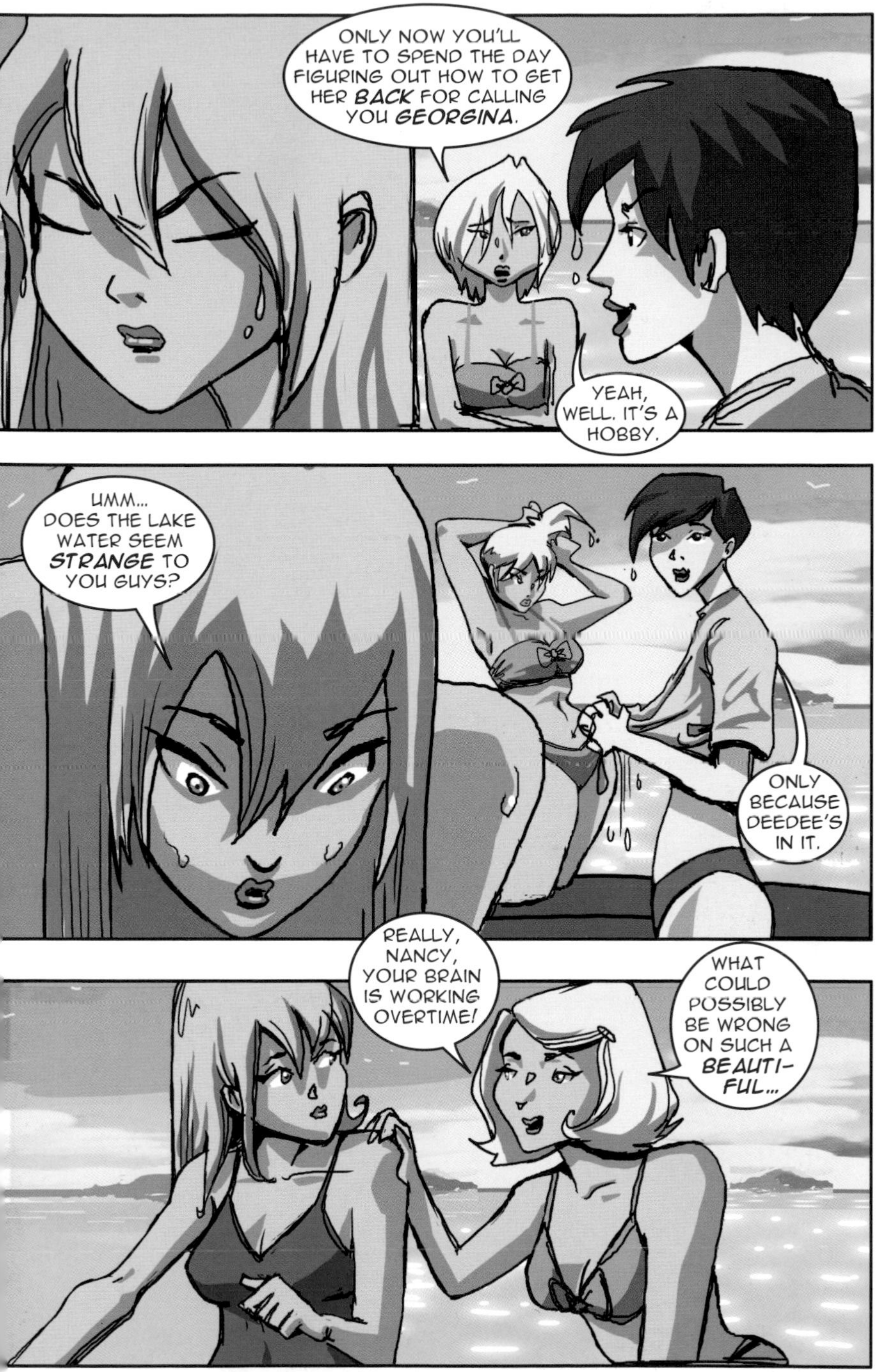
ONLY NOW YOU'LL HAVE TO SPEND THE DAY FIGURING OUT HOW TO GET HER BACK FOR CALLING YOU GEORGINA.
YEAH, WELL. IT'S A HOBBY.
UMM... DOES THE LAKE WATER SEEM STRANGE TO YOU GUYS?
ONLY BECAUSE DEEDEE'S IN IT.
REALLY, NANCY, YOUR BRAIN IS WORKING OVERTIME!
WHAT COULD POSSIBLY BE WRONG ON SUCH A BEAUTI-FUL...

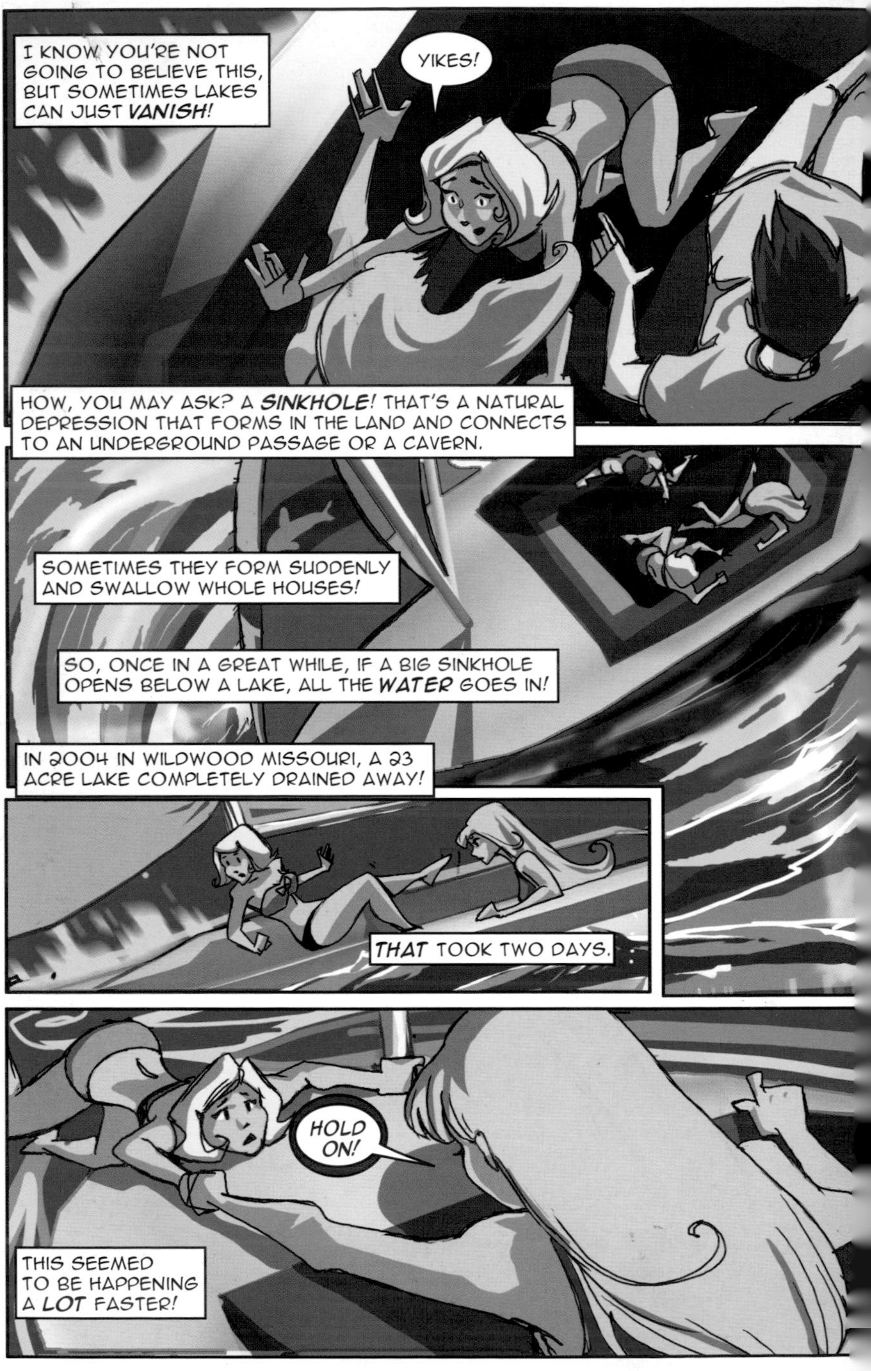

I KNOW YOU'RE NOT GOING TO BELIEVE THIS, BUT SOMETIMES LAKES CAN JUST VANISH!
YIKES!
HOW, YOU MAY ASK? A SINKHOLE! THAT'S A NATURAL DEPRESSION THAT FORMS IN THE LAND AND CONNECTS TO AN UNDERGROUND PASSAGE OR A CAVERN.
SOMETIMES THEY FORM SUDDENLY AND SWALLOW WHOLE HOUSES!
SO, ONCE IN A GREAT WHILE, IF A BIG SINKHOLE OPENS BELOW A LAKE, ALL THE WATER GOES IN!
IN 2004 IN WILDWOOD MISSOURI, A 23 ACRE LAKE COMPLETELY DRAINED AWAY!
THAT TOOK TWO DAYS.
HOLD ON!
THIS SEEMED TO BE HAPPENING A LOT FASTER!

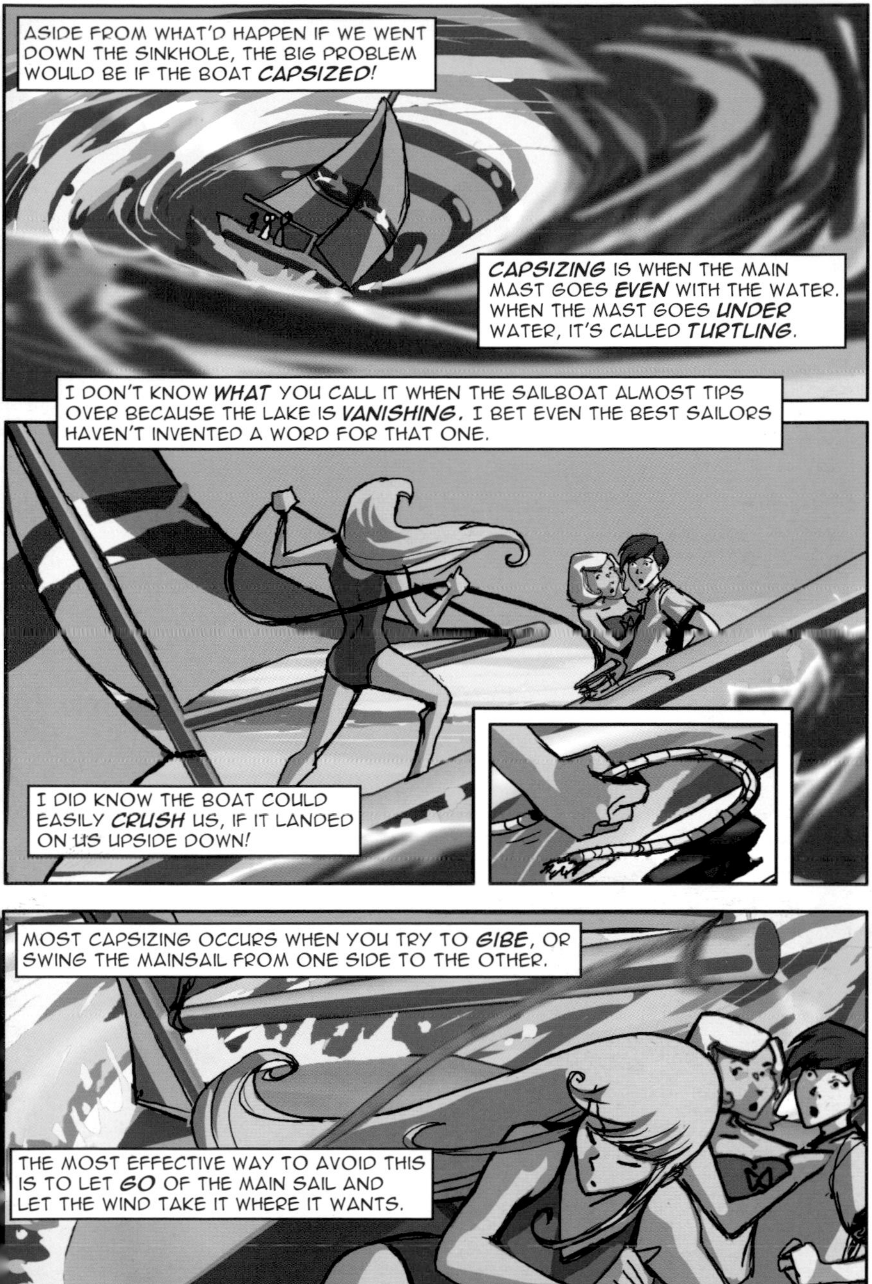
ASIDE FROM WHAT'D HAPPEN IF WE WENT DOWN THE SINKHOLE, THE BIG PROBLEM WOULD BE IF THE BOAT CAPSIZED!
CAPSIZING IS WHEN THE MAIN MAST GOES EVEN WITH THE WATER. WHEN THE MAST GOES UNDER WATER, IT'S CALLED TURTLING.
I DON'T KNOW WHAT YOU CALL IT WHEN THE SAILBOAT ALMOST TIPS OVER BECAUSE THE LAKE IS VANISHING. I BET EVEN THE BEST SAILORS HAVEN'T INVENTED A WORD FOR THAT ONE.
I DID KNOW THE BOAT COULD EASILY CRUSH US, IF IT LANDED ON US UPSIDE DOWN!
MOST CAPSIZING OCCURS WHEN YOU TRY TO GIBE, OR SWING THE MAINSAIL FROM ONE SIDE TO THE OTHER.
THE MOST EFFECTIVE WAY TO AVOID THIS IS TO LET GO OF THE MAIN SAIL AND LET THE WIND TAKE IT WHERE IT WANTS.
THEN GET THE HECK OUT OF ITS WAY!

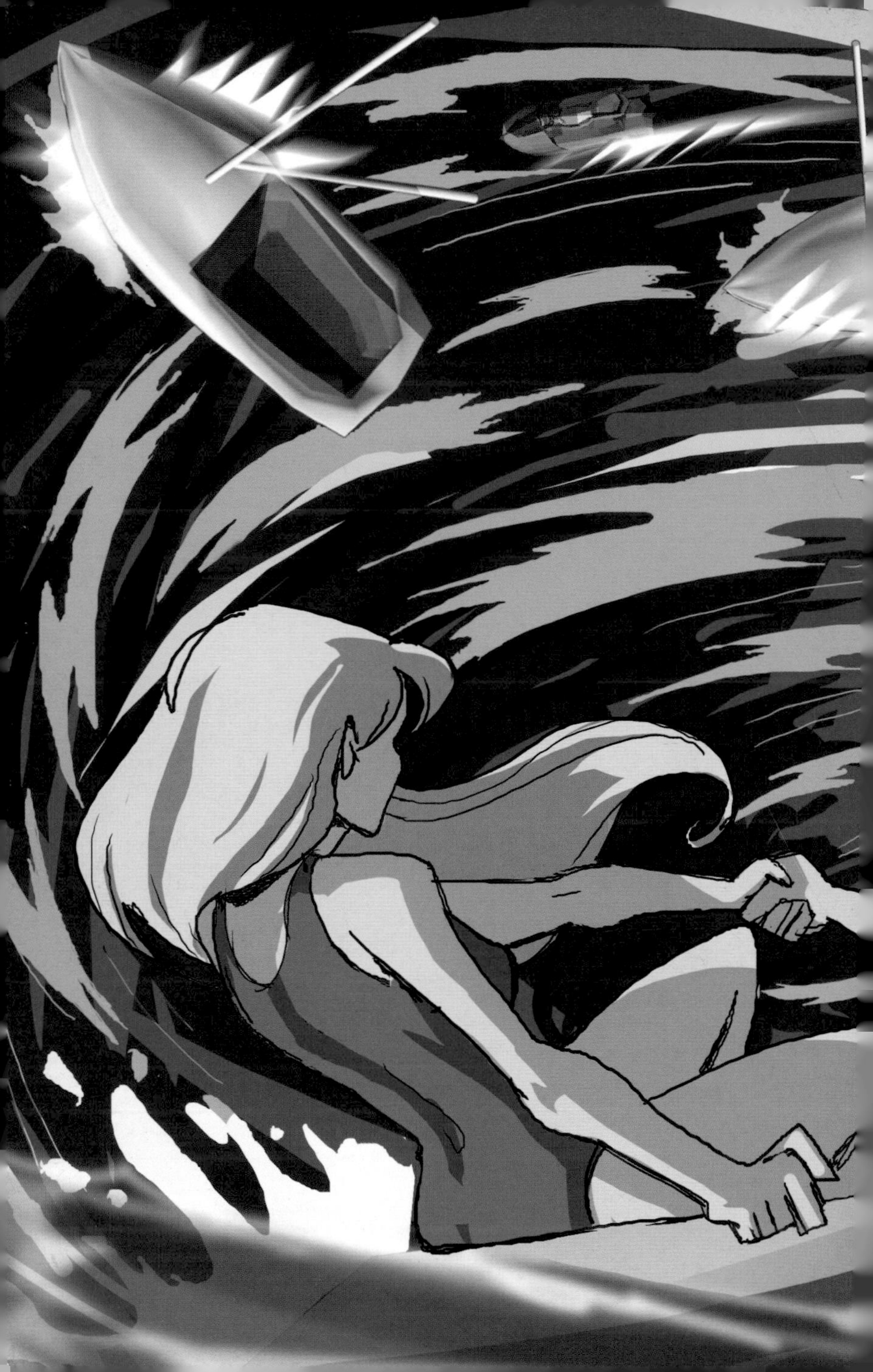

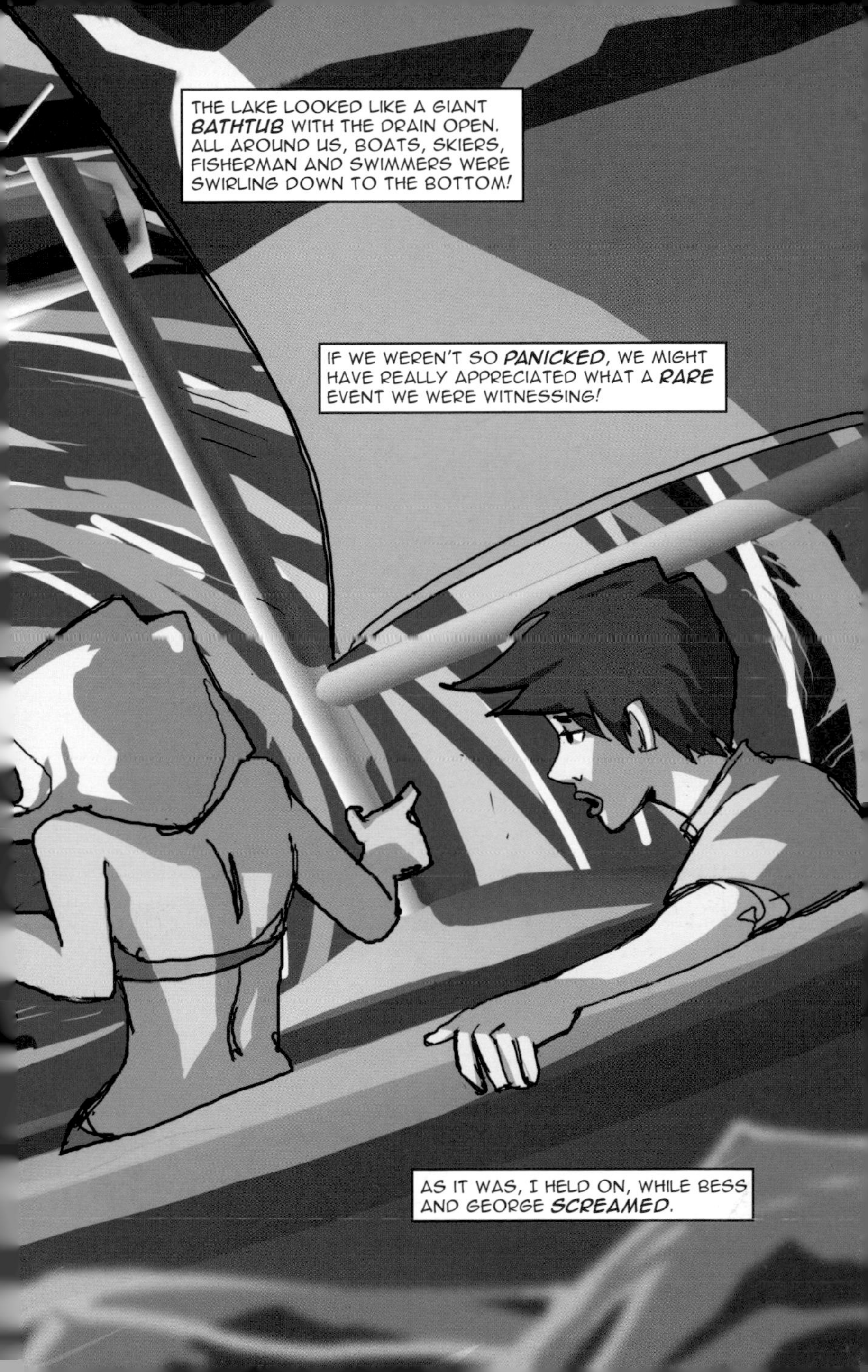
THE LAKE LOOKED LIKE A GIANT BATHTUB WITH THE DRAIN OPEN. ALL AROUND US, BOATS, SKIERS, FISHERMAN AND SWIMMERS WERE SWIRLING DOWN TO THE BOTTOM!
IF WE WEREN'T SO PANICKED, WE MIGHT HAVE REALLY APPRECIATED WHAT A RARE EVENT WE WERE WITNESSING!
AS IT WAS, I HELD ON, WHILE BESS AND GEORGE SCREAMED.

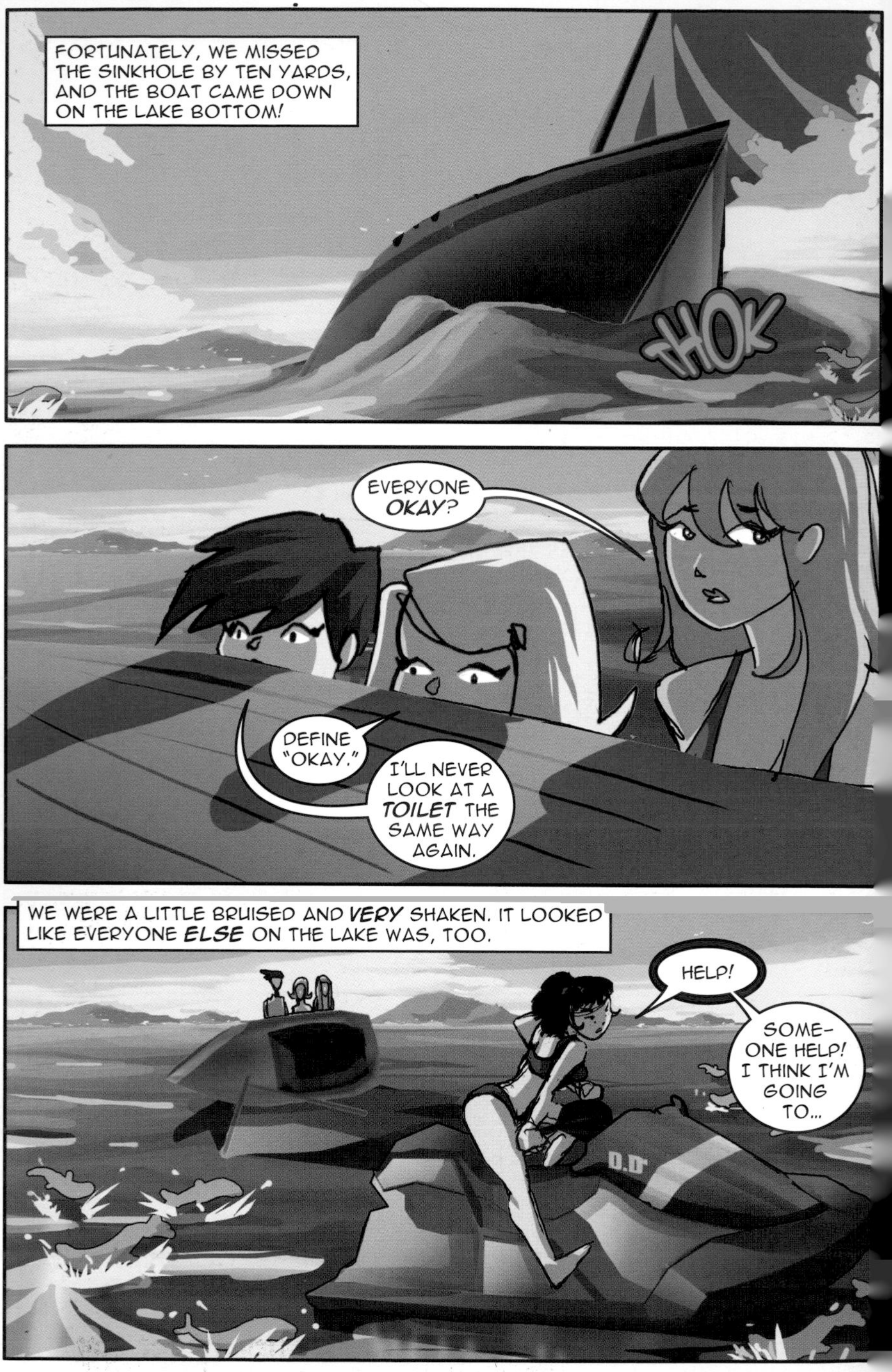
FORTUNATELY, WE MISSED THE SINKHOLE BY TEN YARDS, AND THE BOAT CAME DOWN ON THE LAKE BOTTOM!
THOK
EVERYONE OKAY?
DEFINE "OKAY."
I'LL NEVER LOOK AT A TOILET THE SAME WAY AGAIN.
WE WERE A LITTLE BRUISED AND VERY SHAKEN. IT LOOKED LIKE EVERYONE ELSE ON THE LAKE WAS, TOO.
HELP!
SOME-ONE HELP! I THINK I'M GOING TO...

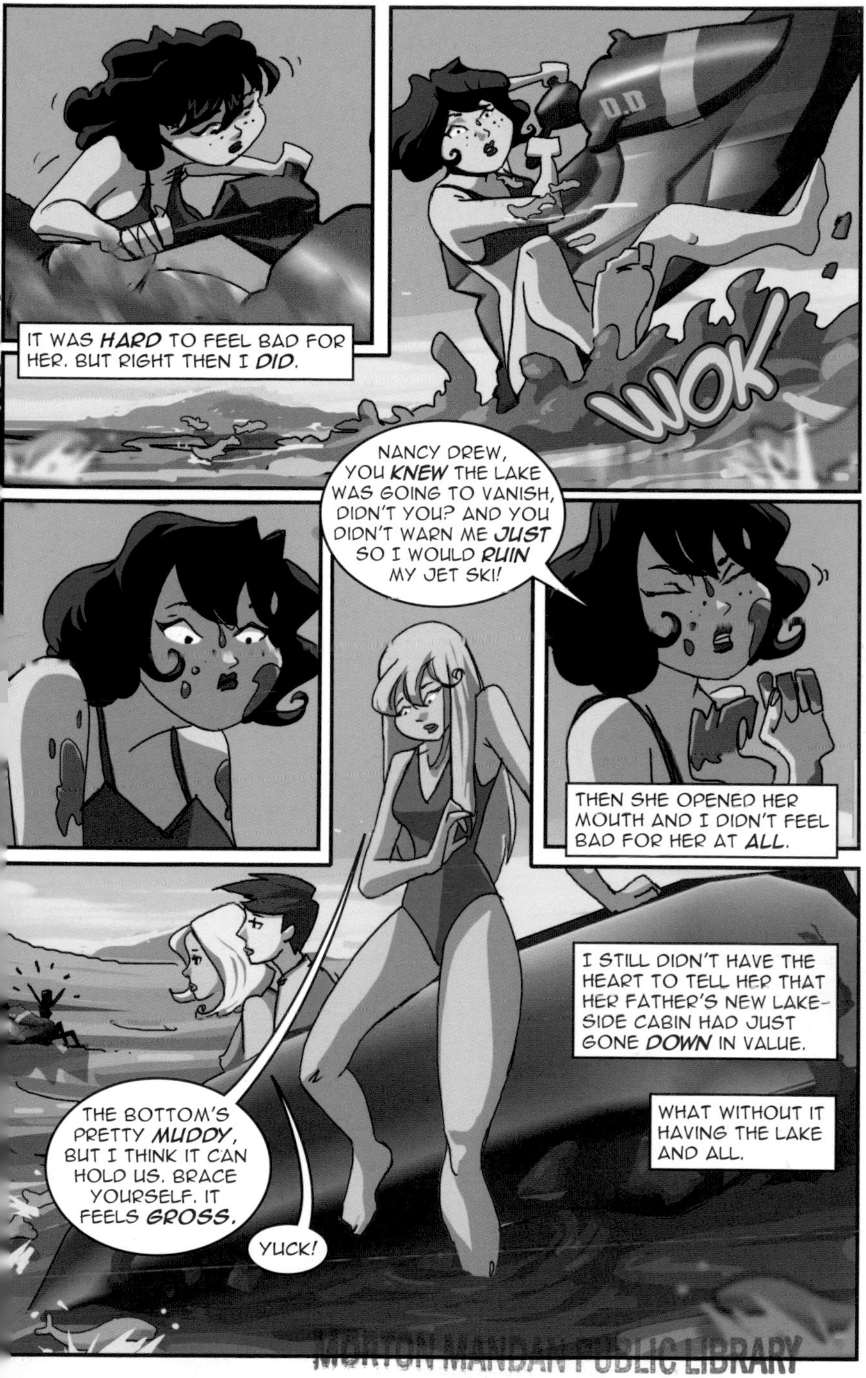
IT WAS HARD TO FEEL BAD FOR HER. BUT RIGHT THEN I DID.
WOK
NANCY DREW, YOU KNEW THE LAKE WAS GOING TO VANISH, DIDN'T YOU? AND YOU DIDN'T WARN ME JUST SO I WOULD RUIN MY JET SKI!
THEN SHE OPENED HER MOUTH AND I DIDN'T FEEL BAD FOR HER AT ALL.
I STILL DIDN'T HAVE THE HEART TO TELL HER THAT HER FATHER'S NEW LAKE-SIDE CABIN HAD JUST GONE DOWN IN VALUE.
WHAT WITHOUT IT HAVING THE LAKE AND ALL.
THE BOTTOM'S PRETTY MUDDY, BUT I THINK IT CAN HOLD US. BRACE YOURSELF. IT FEELS GROSS.
YUCK!

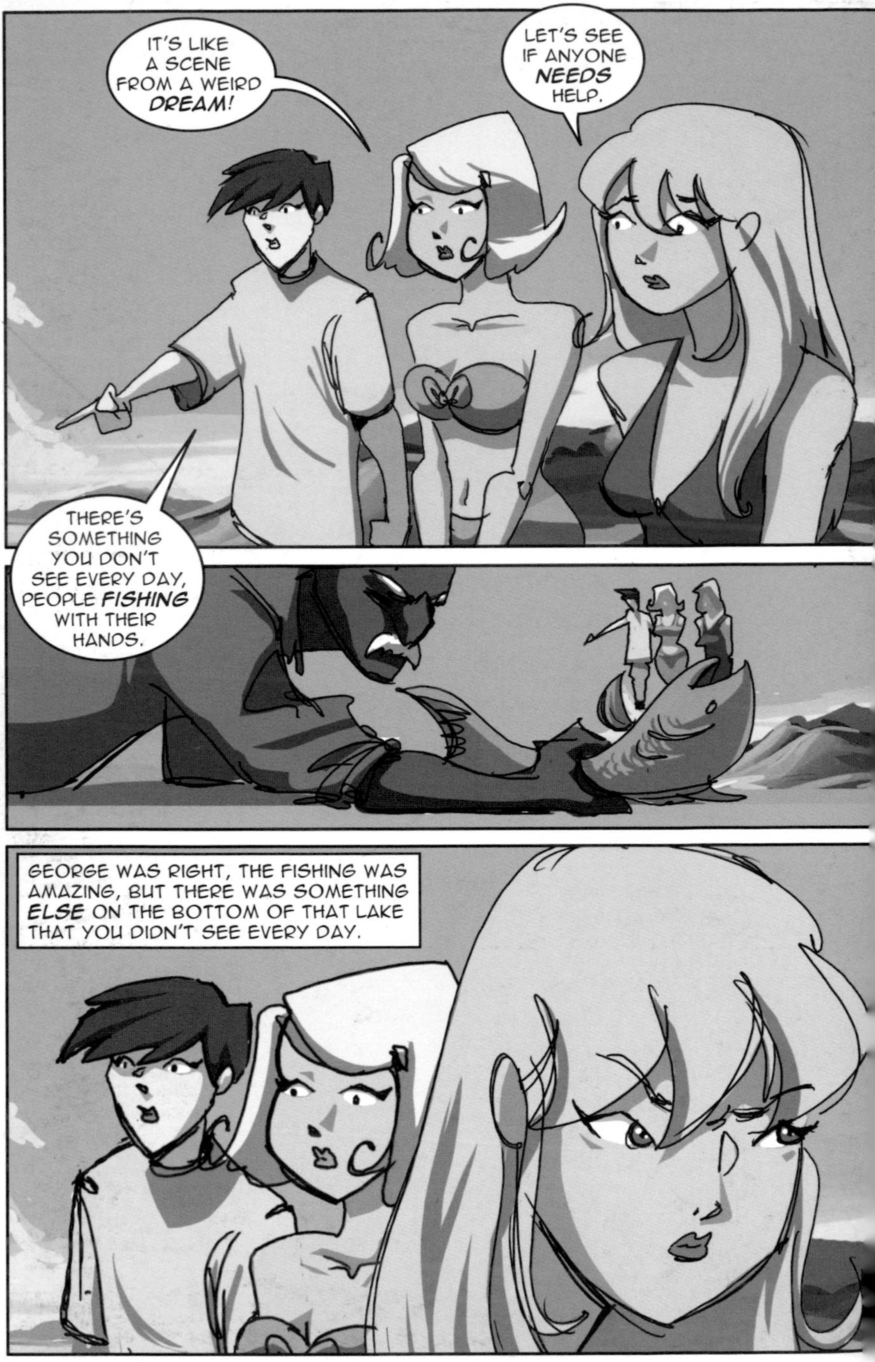
IT'S LIKE A SCENE FROM A WEIRD DREAM!
LET'S SEE IF ANYONE NEEDS HELP.
THERE'S SOMETHING YOU DON'T SEE EVERY DAY, PEOPLE FISHING WITH THEIR HANDS.
GEORGE WAS RIGHT, THE FISHING WAS AMAZING, BUT THERE WAS SOMETHING ELSE ON THE BOTTOM OF THAT LAKE THAT YOU DIDN'T SEE EVERY DAY.

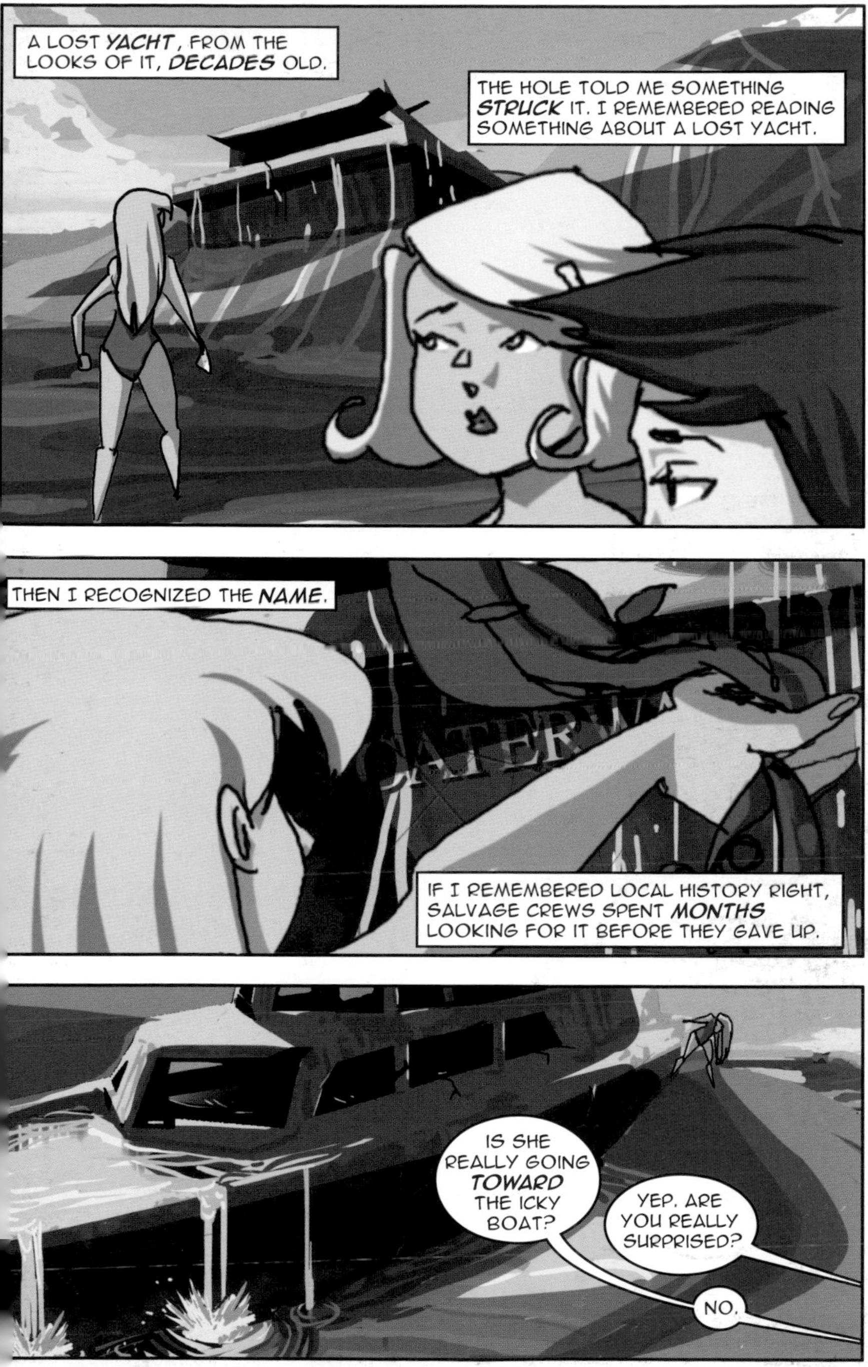
A LOST *YACHT*, FROM THE LOOKS OF IT, *DECADES* OLD.
THE HOLE TOLD ME SOMETHING *STRUCK* IT. I REMEMBERED READING SOMETHING ABOUT A LOST YACHT.
THEN I RECOGNIZED THE *NAME*.
IF I REMEMBERED LOCAL HISTORY RIGHT, SALVAGE CREWS SPENT *MONTHS* LOOKING FOR IT BEFORE THEY GAVE UP.
IS SHE REALLY GOING *TOWARD* THE ICKY BOAT?
YEP. ARE YOU REALLY SURPRISED?
NO.

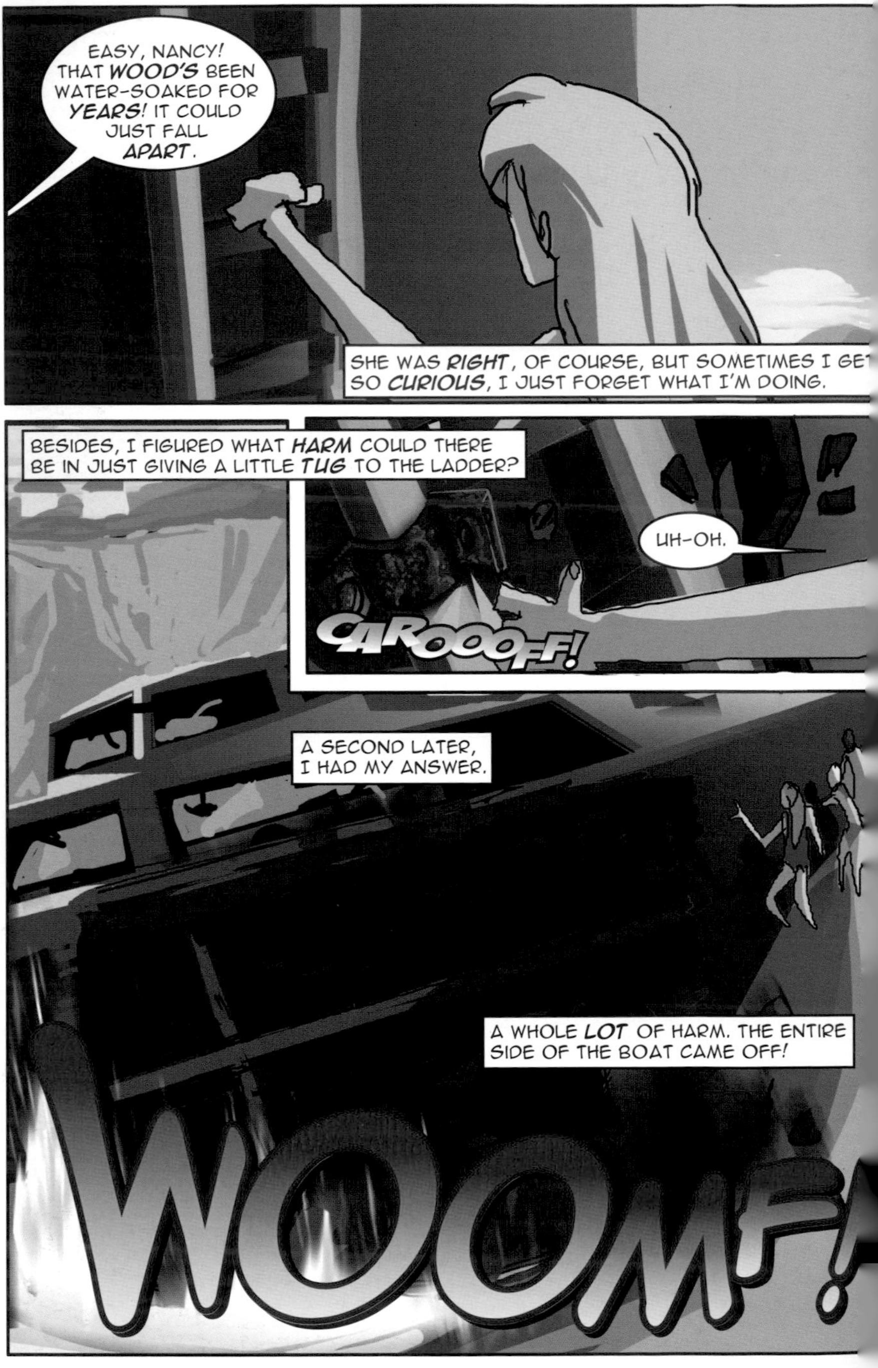
EASY, NANCY! THAT WOOD'S BEEN WATER-SOAKED FOR YEARS! IT COULD JUST FALL APART.
SHE WAS RIGHT, OF COURSE, BUT SOMETIMES I GET SO CURIOUS, I JUST FORGET WHAT I'M DOING.
BESIDES, I FIGURED WHAT HARM COULD THERE BE IN JUST GIVING A LITTLE TUG TO THE LADDER?
UH-OH.
CAROOOFF!
A SECOND LATER, I HAD MY ANSWER.
A WHOLE LOT OF HARM. THE ENTIRE SIDE OF THE BOAT CAME OFF!
WOOMF!

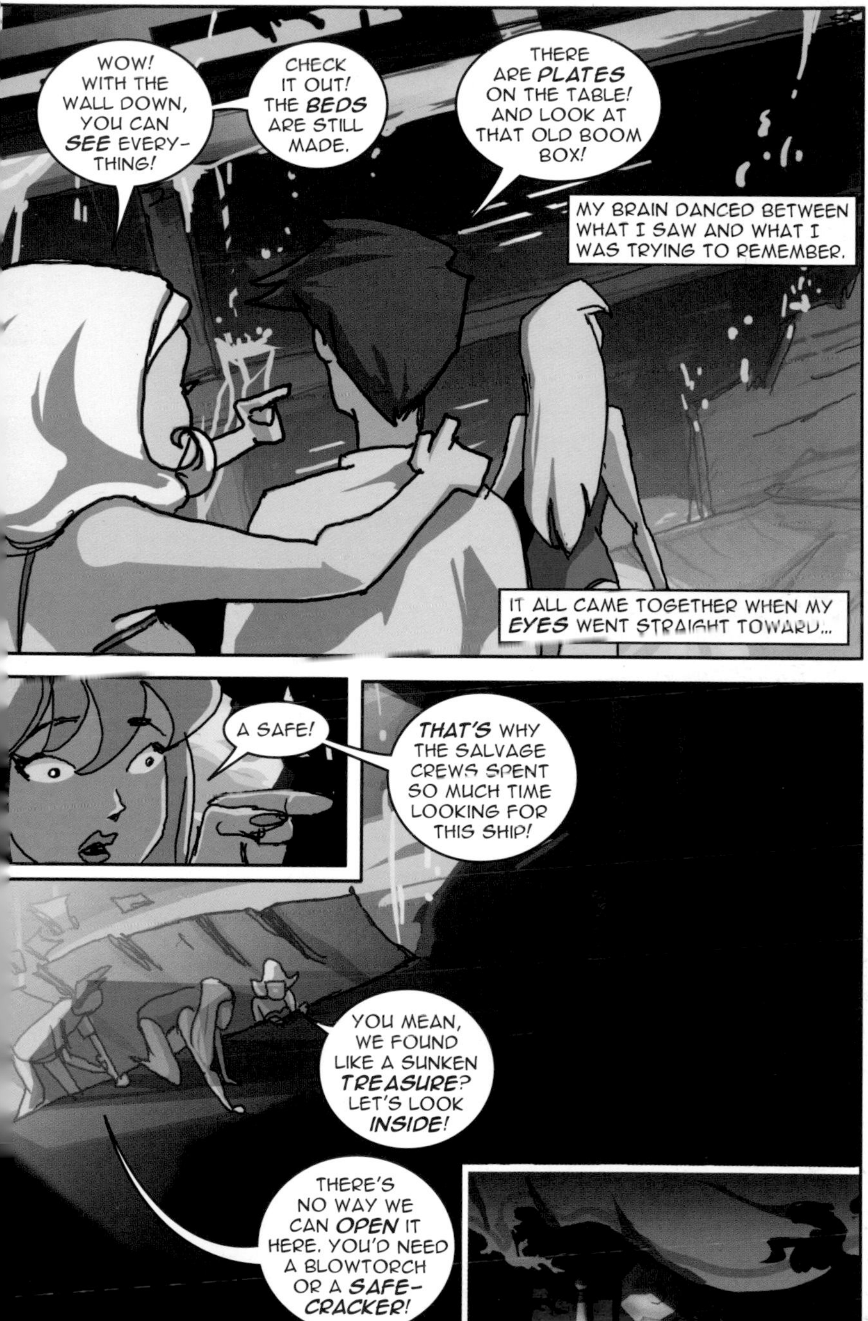
WOW! WITH THE WALL DOWN, YOU CAN SEE EVERYTHING!
CHECK IT OUT! THE BEDS ARE STILL MADE.
THERE ARE PLATES ON THE TABLE! AND LOOK AT THAT OLD BOOM BOX!
MY BRAIN DANCED BETWEEN WHAT I SAW AND WHAT I WAS TRYING TO REMEMBER.
IT ALL CAME TOGETHER WHEN MY EYES WENT STRAIGHT TOWARD...
A SAFE!
THAT'S WHY THE SALVAGE CREWS SPENT SO MUCH TIME LOOKING FOR THIS SHIP!
YOU MEAN, WE FOUND LIKE A SUNKEN TREASURE? LET'S LOOK INSIDE!
THERE'S NO WAY WE CAN OPEN IT HERE. YOU'D NEED A BLOWTORCH OR A SAFE-CRACKER!

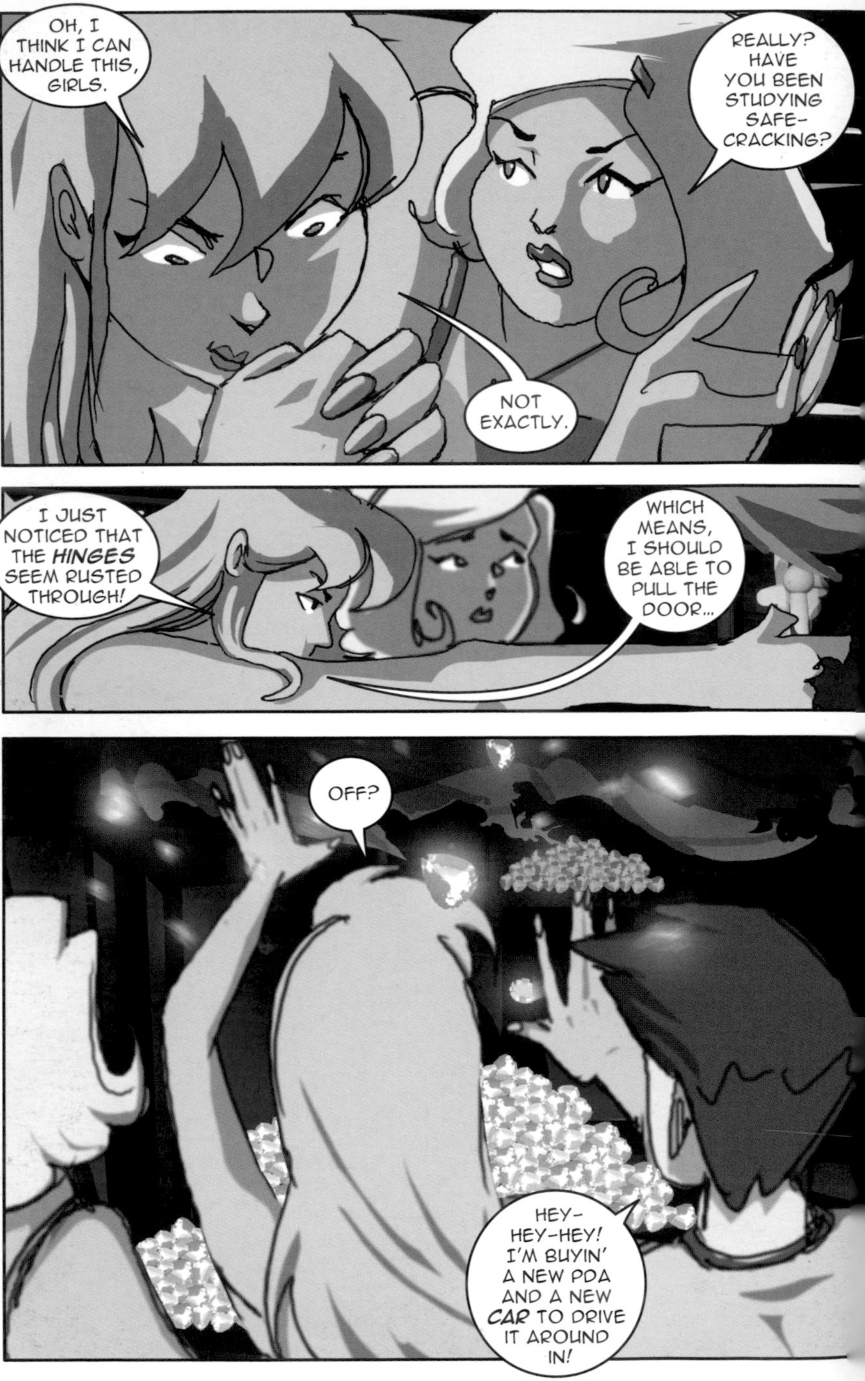
OH, I THINK I CAN HANDLE THIS, GIRLS.
REALLY? HAVE YOU BEEN STUDYING SAFE-CRACKING?
NOT EXACTLY.
I JUST NOTICED THAT THE HINGES SEEM RUSTED THROUGH!
WHICH MEANS, I SHOULD BE ABLE TO PULL THE DOOR...
OFF?
HEY-HEY-HEY! I'M BUYIN' A NEW PDA AND A NEW CAR TO DRIVE IT AROUND IN!

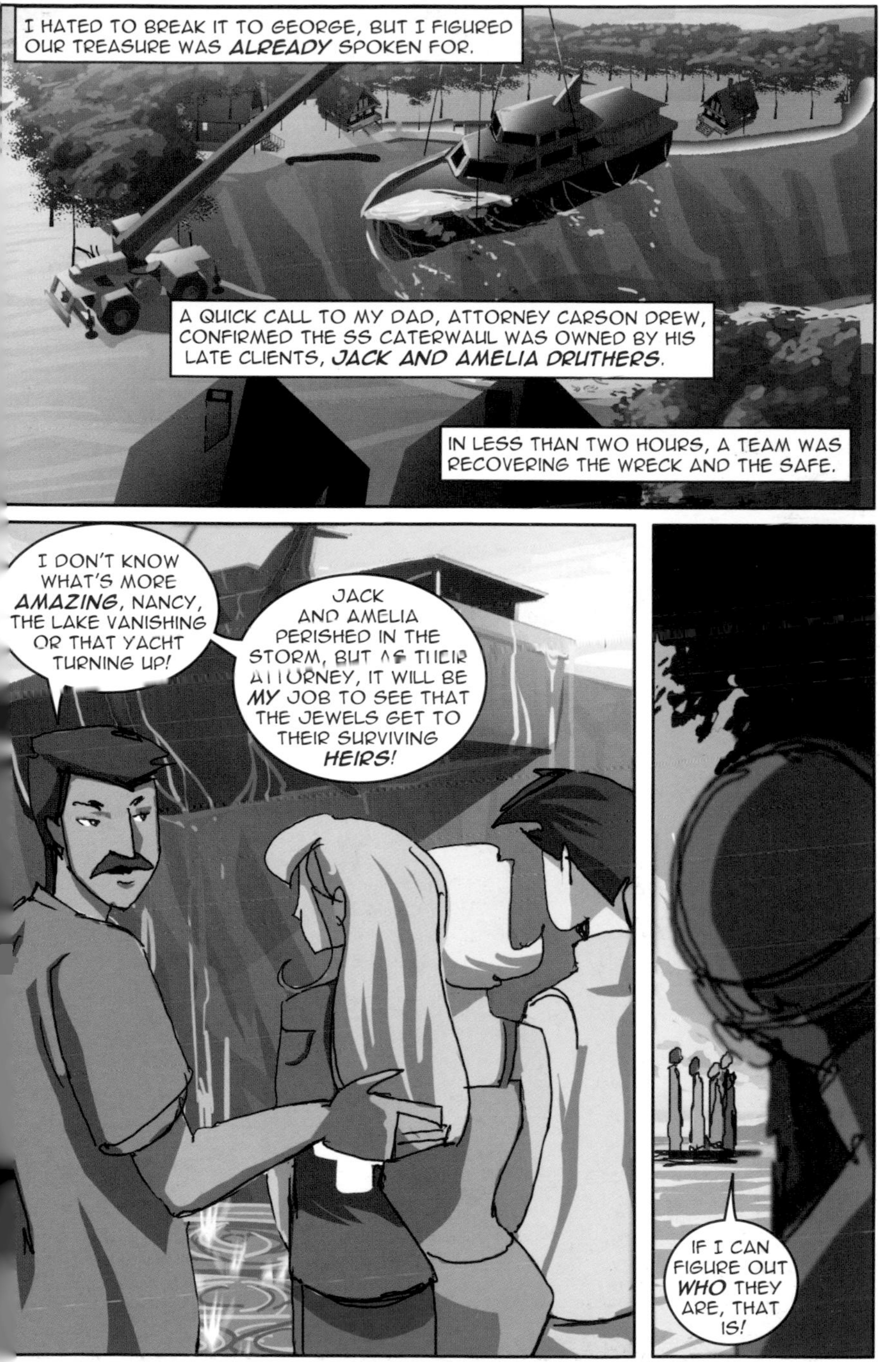
I HATED TO BREAK IT TO GEORGE, BUT I FIGURED OUR TREASURE WAS ALREADY SPOKEN FOR.
A QUICK CALL TO MY DAD, ATTORNEY CARSON DREW, CONFIRMED THE SS CATERWAUL WAS OWNED BY HIS LATE CLIENTS, JACK AND AMELIA DRUTHERS.
IN LESS THAN TWO HOURS, A TEAM WAS RECOVERING THE WRECK AND THE SAFE.
I DON'T KNOW WHAT'S MORE AMAZING, NANCY, THE LAKE VANISHING OR THAT YACHT TURNING UP!
JACK AND AMELIA PERISHED IN THE STORM, BUT AS THEIR ATTORNEY, IT WILL BE MY JOB TO SEE THAT THE JEWELS GET TO THEIR SURVIVING HEIRS!
IF I CAN FIGURE OUT WHO THEY ARE, THAT IS!

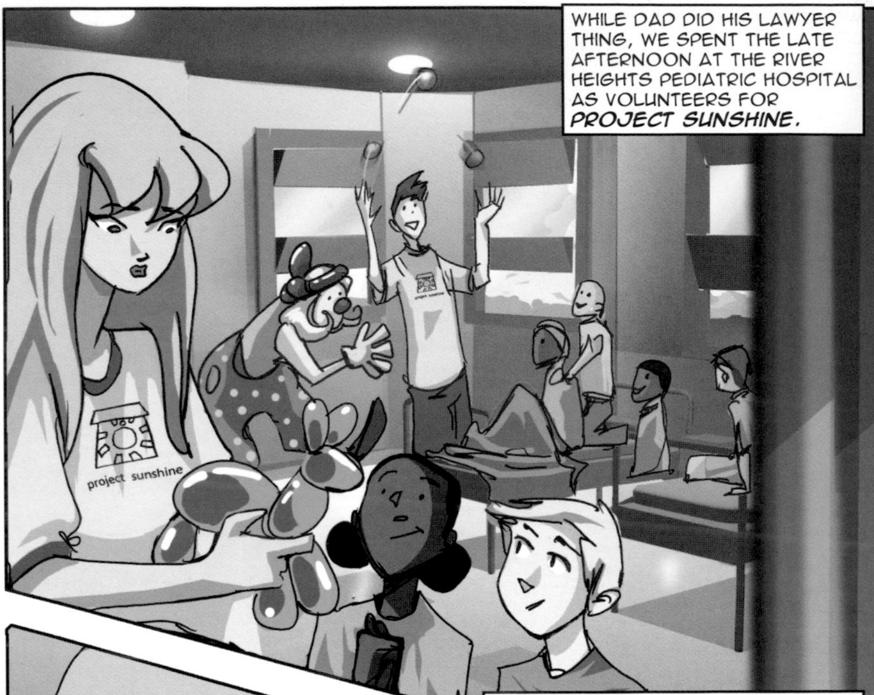
WHILE DAD DID HIS LAWYER THING, WE SPENT THE LATE AFTERNOON AT THE RIVER HEIGHTS PEDIATRIC HOSPITAL AS VOLUNTEERS FOR *PROJECT SUNSHINE.*
project sunshine

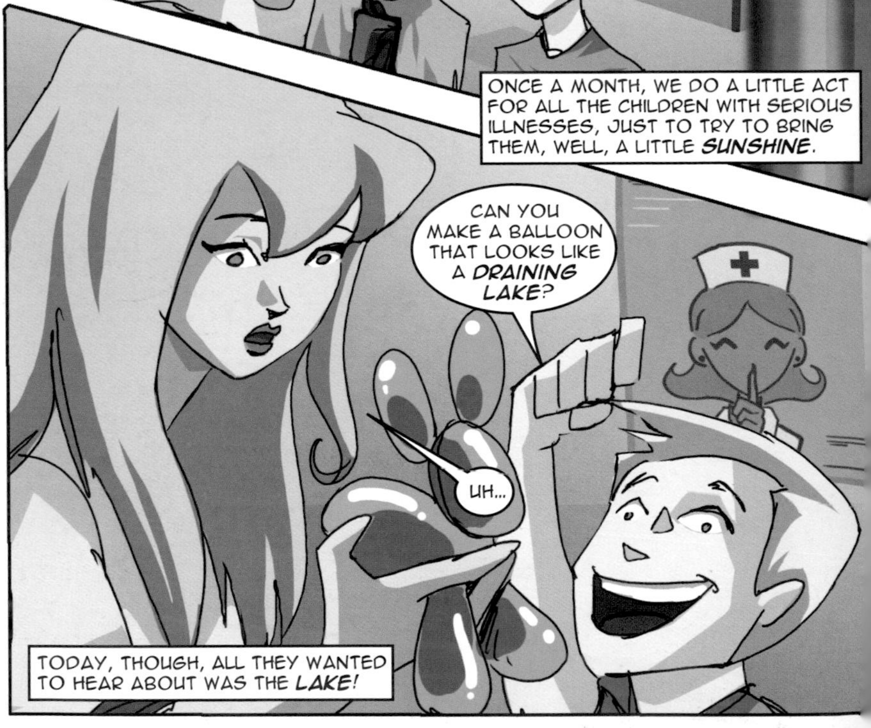
ONCE A MONTH, WE DO A LITTLE ACT FOR ALL THE CHILDREN WITH SERIOUS ILLNESSES, JUST TO TRY TO BRING THEM, WELL, A LITTLE *SUNSHINE*.
CAN YOU MAKE A BALLOON THAT LOOKS LIKE A *DRAINING LAKE*?
UH...
TODAY, THOUGH, ALL THEY WANTED TO HEAR ABOUT WAS THE *LAKE!*

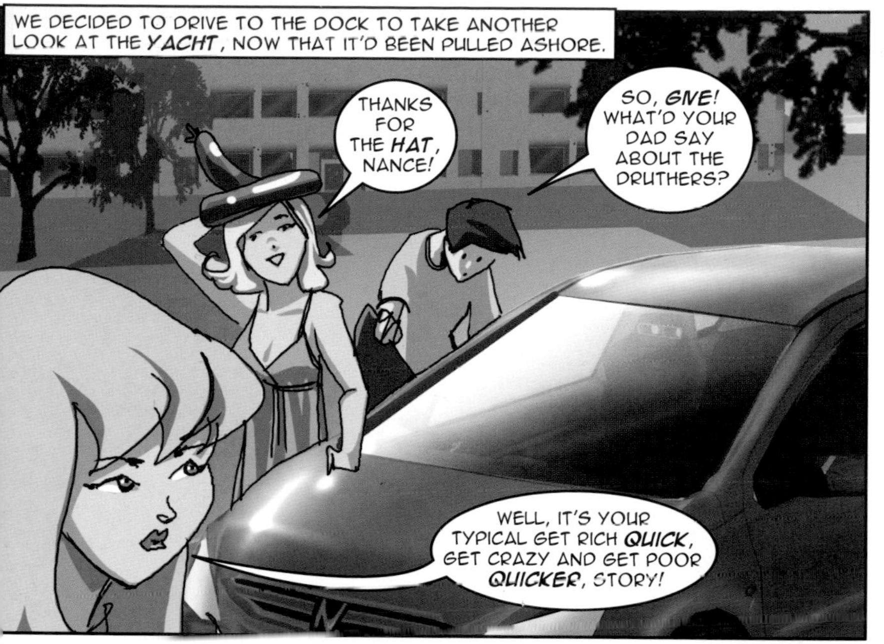
WE DECIDED TO DRIVE TO THE DOCK TO TAKE ANOTHER LOOK AT THE *YACHT*, NOW THAT IT'D BEEN PULLED ASHORE.
THANKS FOR THE *HAT*, NANCE!
SO, *GIVE*! WHAT'D YOUR DAD SAY ABOUT THE DRUTHERS?
WELL, IT'S YOUR TYPICAL GET RICH **QUICK**, GET CRAZY AND GET POOR **QUICKER**, STORY!

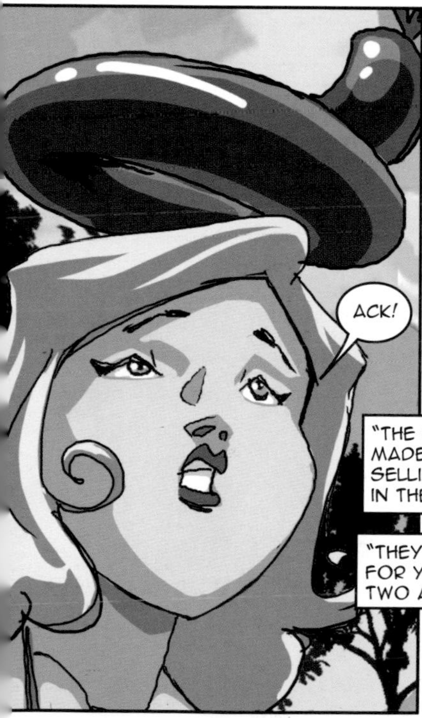
ACK!
"THE DRUTHERS MADE A FORTUNE SELLING FAX PAPER IN THE EARLY 1980s."
"THEY LIVED THE GOOD LIFE FOR YEARS, LIMOS, ESTATES, TWO AIRPLANES."

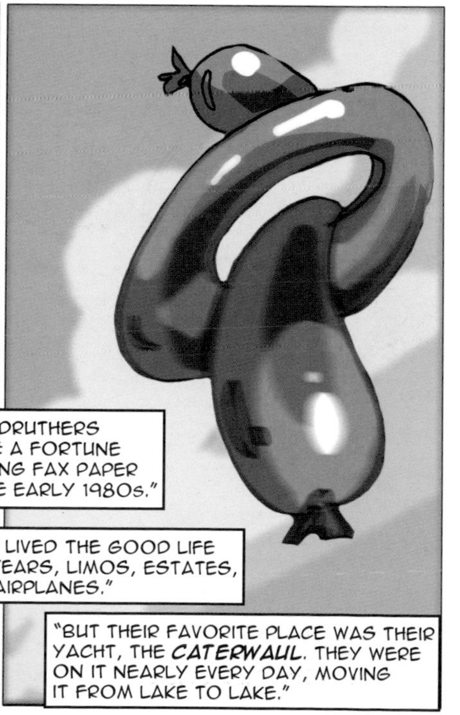
"BUT THEIR FAVORITE PLACE WAS THEIR YACHT, THE **CATERWAUL**. THEY WERE ON IT NEARLY EVERY DAY, MOVING IT FROM LAKE TO LAKE."

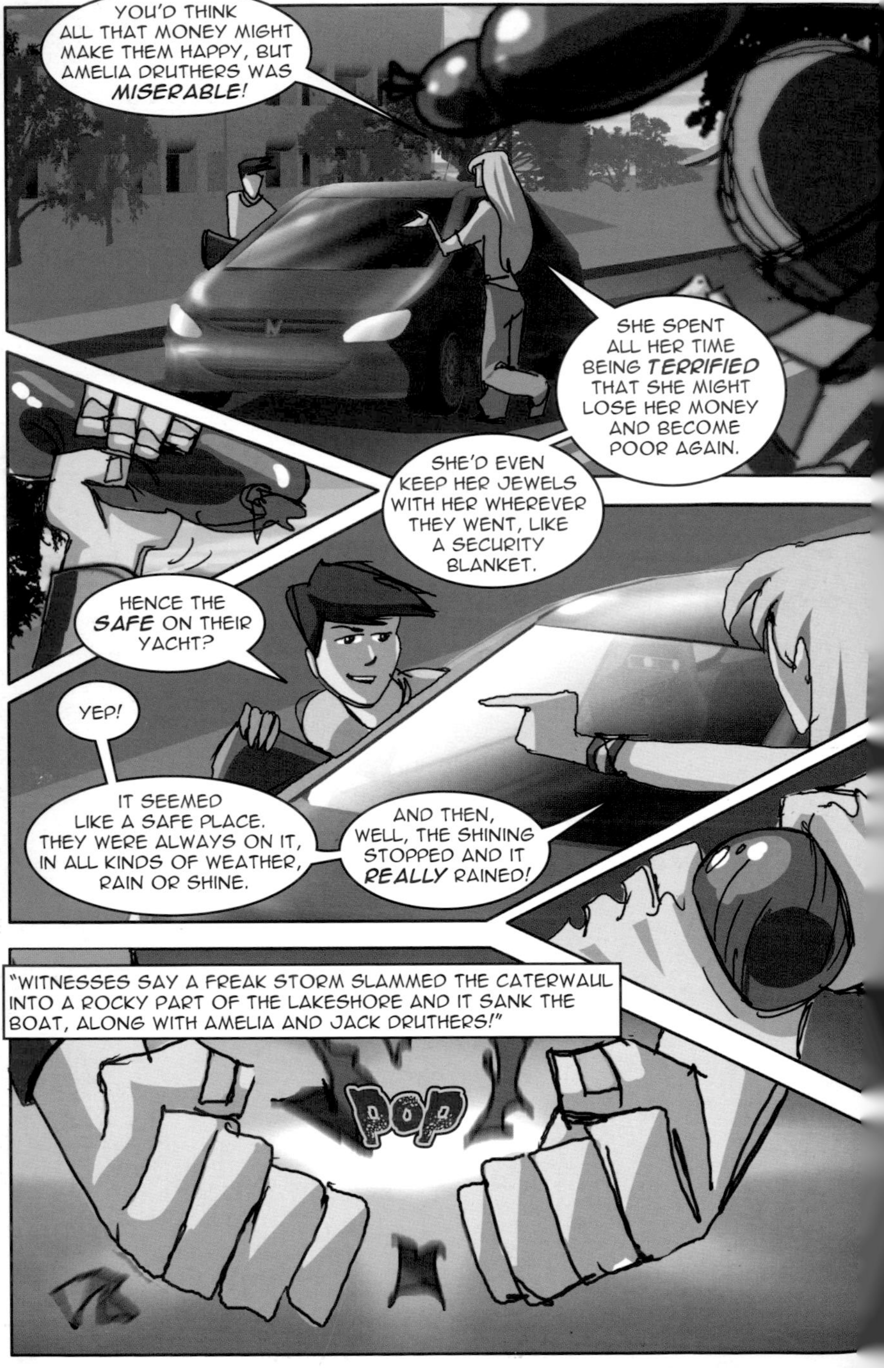
YOU'D THINK ALL THAT MONEY MIGHT MAKE THEM HAPPY, BUT AMELIA DRUTHERS WAS *MISERABLE*!
SHE SPENT ALL HER TIME BEING *TERRIFIED* THAT SHE MIGHT LOSE HER MONEY AND BECOME POOR AGAIN.
SHE'D EVEN KEEP HER JEWELS WITH HER WHEREVER THEY WENT, LIKE A SECURITY BLANKET.
HENCE THE *SAFE* ON THEIR YACHT?
YEP!
IT SEEMED LIKE A SAFE PLACE. THEY WERE ALWAYS ON IT, IN ALL KINDS OF WEATHER, RAIN OR SHINE.
AND THEN, WELL, THE SHINING STOPPED AND IT *REALLY* RAINED!
"WITNESSES SAY A FREAK STORM SLAMMED THE CATERWAUL INTO A ROCKY PART OF THE LAKESHORE AND IT SANK THE BOAT, ALONG WITH AMELIA AND JACK DRUTHERS!"
POP

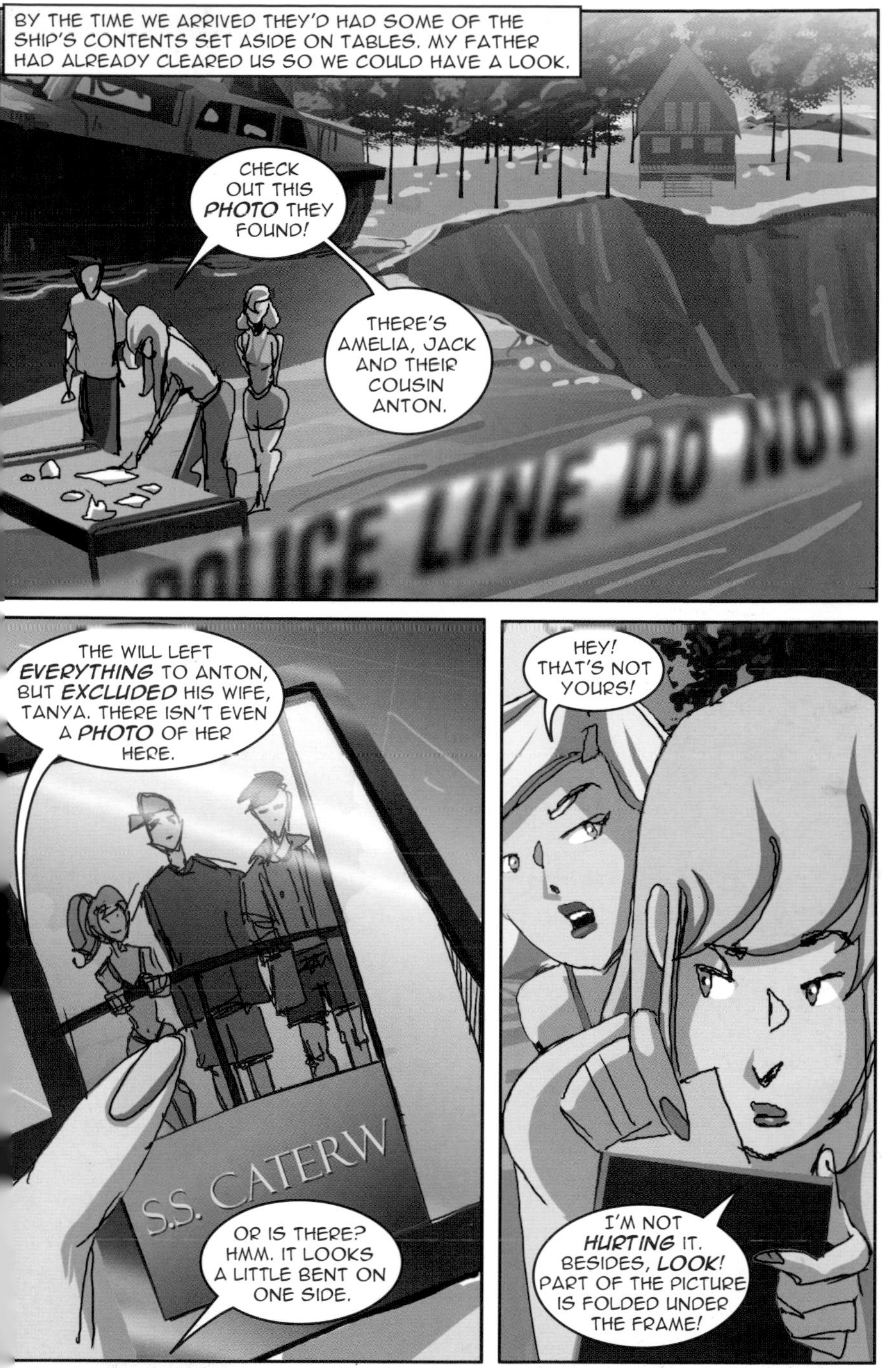
BY THE TIME WE ARRIVED THEY'D HAD SOME OF THE SHIP'S CONTENTS SET ASIDE ON TABLES. MY FATHER HAD ALREADY CLEARED US SO WE COULD HAVE A LOOK.
CHECK OUT THIS PHOTO THEY FOUND!
THERE'S AMELIA, JACK AND THEIR COUSIN ANTON.
POLICE LINE DO NOT
THE WILL LEFT EVERYTHING TO ANTON, BUT EXCLUDED HIS WIFE, TANYA. THERE ISN'T EVEN A PHOTO OF HER HERE.
S.S. CATERW
OR IS THERE? HMM. IT LOOKS A LITTLE BENT ON ONE SIDE.
HEY! THAT'S NOT YOURS!
I'M NOT HURTING IT. BESIDES, LOOK! PART OF THE PICTURE IS FOLDED UNDER THE FRAME!

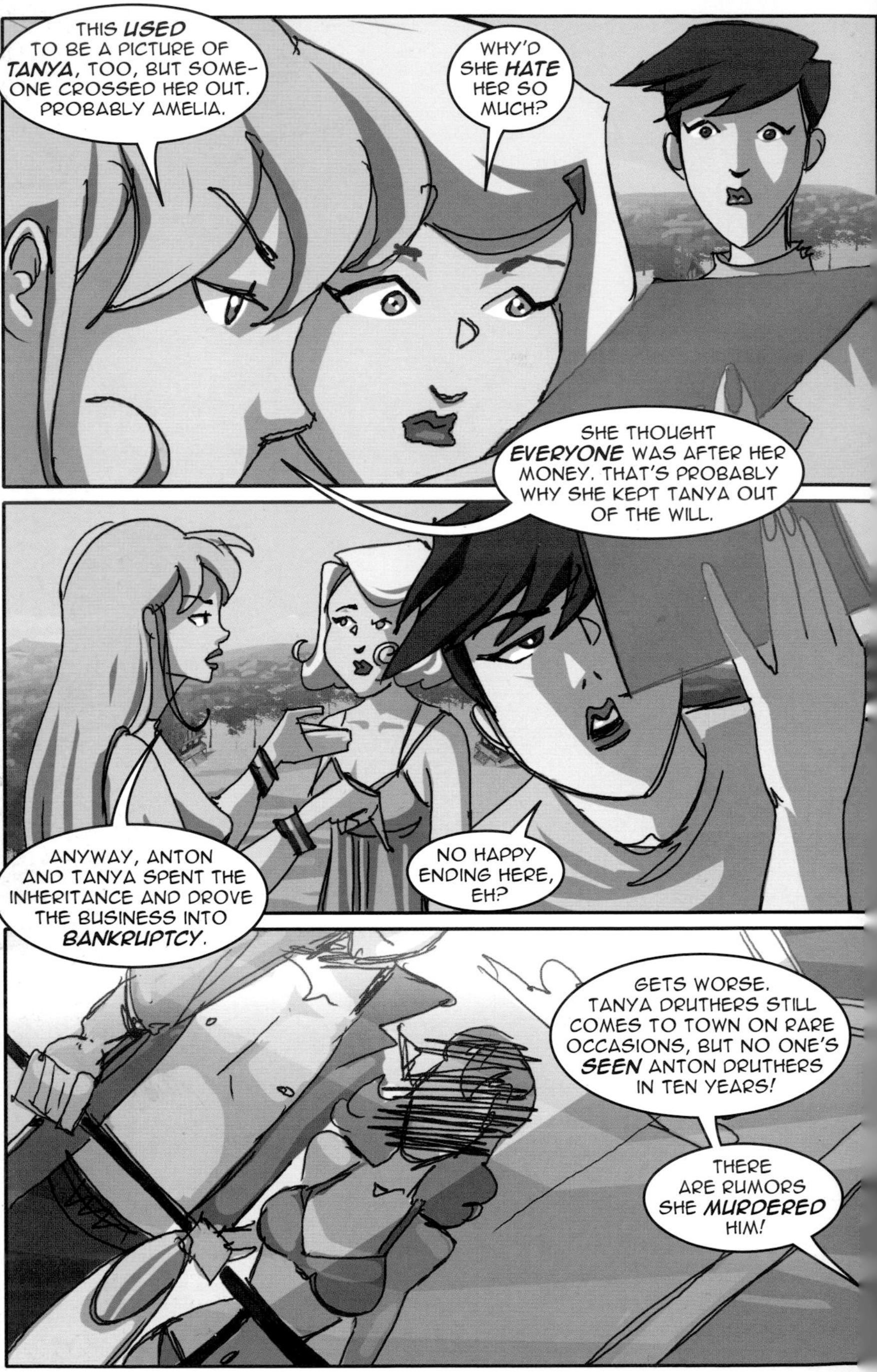
THIS USED TO BE A PICTURE OF TANYA, TOO, BUT SOME-ONE CROSSED HER OUT. PROBABLY AMELIA.
WHY'D SHE HATE HER SO MUCH?
SHE THOUGHT EVERYONE WAS AFTER HER MONEY. THAT'S PROBABLY WHY SHE KEPT TANYA OUT OF THE WILL.
ANYWAY, ANTON AND TANYA SPENT THE INHERITANCE AND DROVE THE BUSINESS INTO BANKRUPTCY.
NO HAPPY ENDING HERE, EH?
GETS WORSE. TANYA DRUTHERS STILL COMES TO TOWN ON RARE OCCASIONS, BUT NO ONE'S SEEN ANTON DRUTHERS IN TEN YEARS!
THERE ARE RUMORS SHE MURDERED HIM!

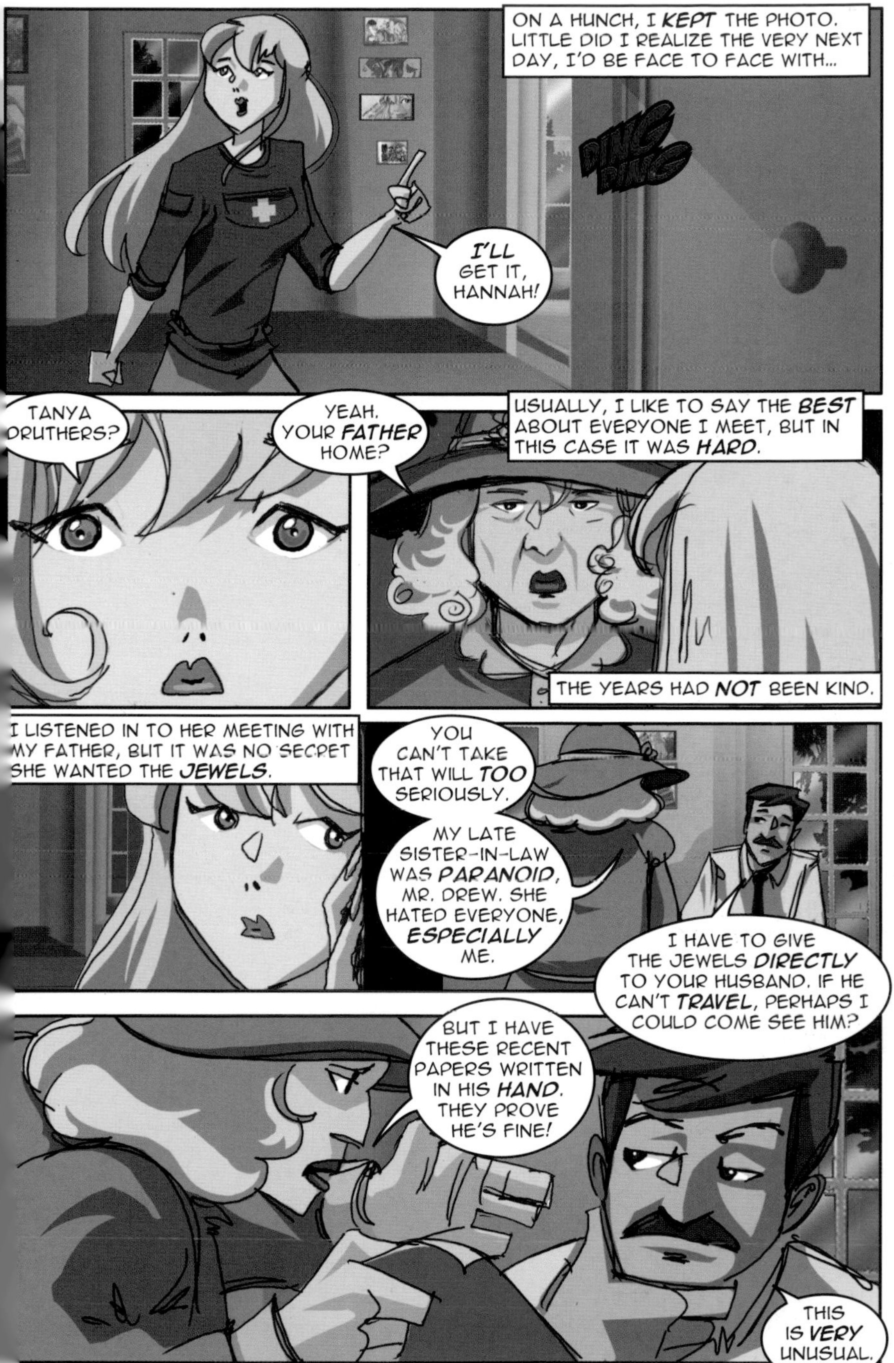

ON A HUNCH, I KEPT THE PHOTO. LITTLE DID I REALIZE THE VERY NEXT DAY, I'D BE FACE TO FACE WITH...
DING DING
I'LL GET IT, HANNAH!
TANYA DRUTHERS?
YEAH. YOUR FATHER HOME?
USUALLY, I LIKE TO SAY THE BEST ABOUT EVERYONE I MEET, BUT IN THIS CASE IT WAS HARD.
THE YEARS HAD NOT BEEN KIND.
I LISTENED IN TO HER MEETING WITH MY FATHER, BUT IT WAS NO SECRET SHE WANTED THE JEWELS.
YOU CAN'T TAKE THAT WILL TOO SERIOUSLY.
MY LATE SISTER-IN-LAW WAS PARANOID, MR. DREW. SHE HATED EVERYONE, ESPECIALLY ME.
I HAVE TO GIVE THE JEWELS DIRECTLY TO YOUR HUSBAND. IF HE CAN'T TRAVEL, PERHAPS I COULD COME SEE HIM?
BUT I HAVE THESE RECENT PAPERS WRITTEN IN HIS HAND. THEY PROVE HE'S FINE!
THIS IS VERY UNUSUAL.

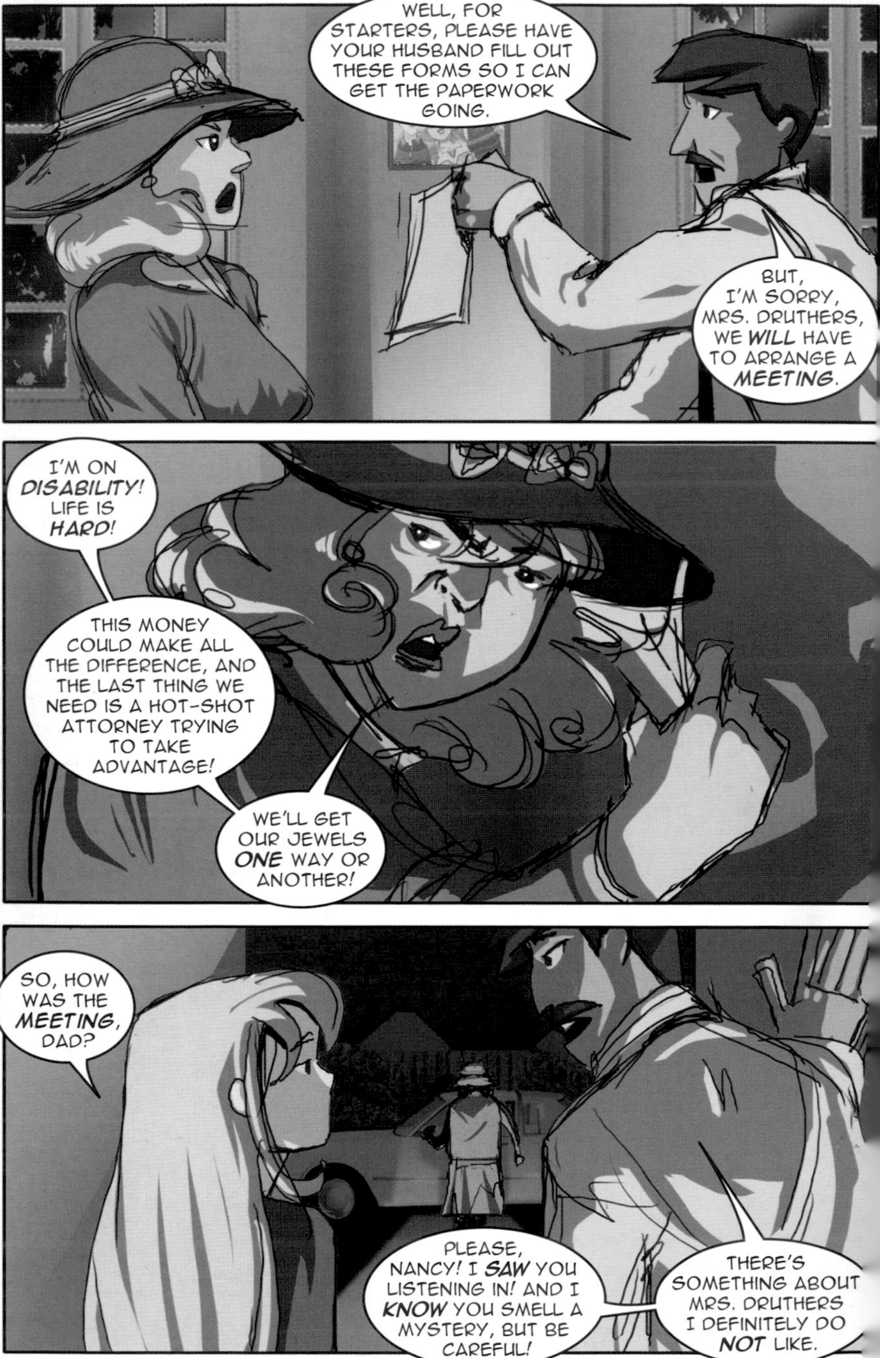
WELL, FOR STARTERS, PLEASE HAVE YOUR HUSBAND FILL OUT THESE FORMS SO I CAN GET THE PAPERWORK GOING.
BUT, I'M SORRY, MRS. DRUTHERS, WE WILL HAVE TO ARRANGE A MEETING.
I'M ON DISABILITY! LIFE IS HARD!
THIS MONEY COULD MAKE ALL THE DIFFERENCE, AND THE LAST THING WE NEED IS A HOT-SHOT ATTORNEY TRYING TO TAKE ADVANTAGE!
WE'LL GET OUR JEWELS ONE WAY OR ANOTHER!
SO, HOW WAS THE MEETING, DAD?
PLEASE, NANCY! I SAW YOU LISTENING IN! AND I KNOW YOU SMELL A MYSTERY, BUT BE CAREFUL!
THERE'S SOMETHING ABOUT MRS. DRUTHERS I DEFINITELY DO NOT LIKE.

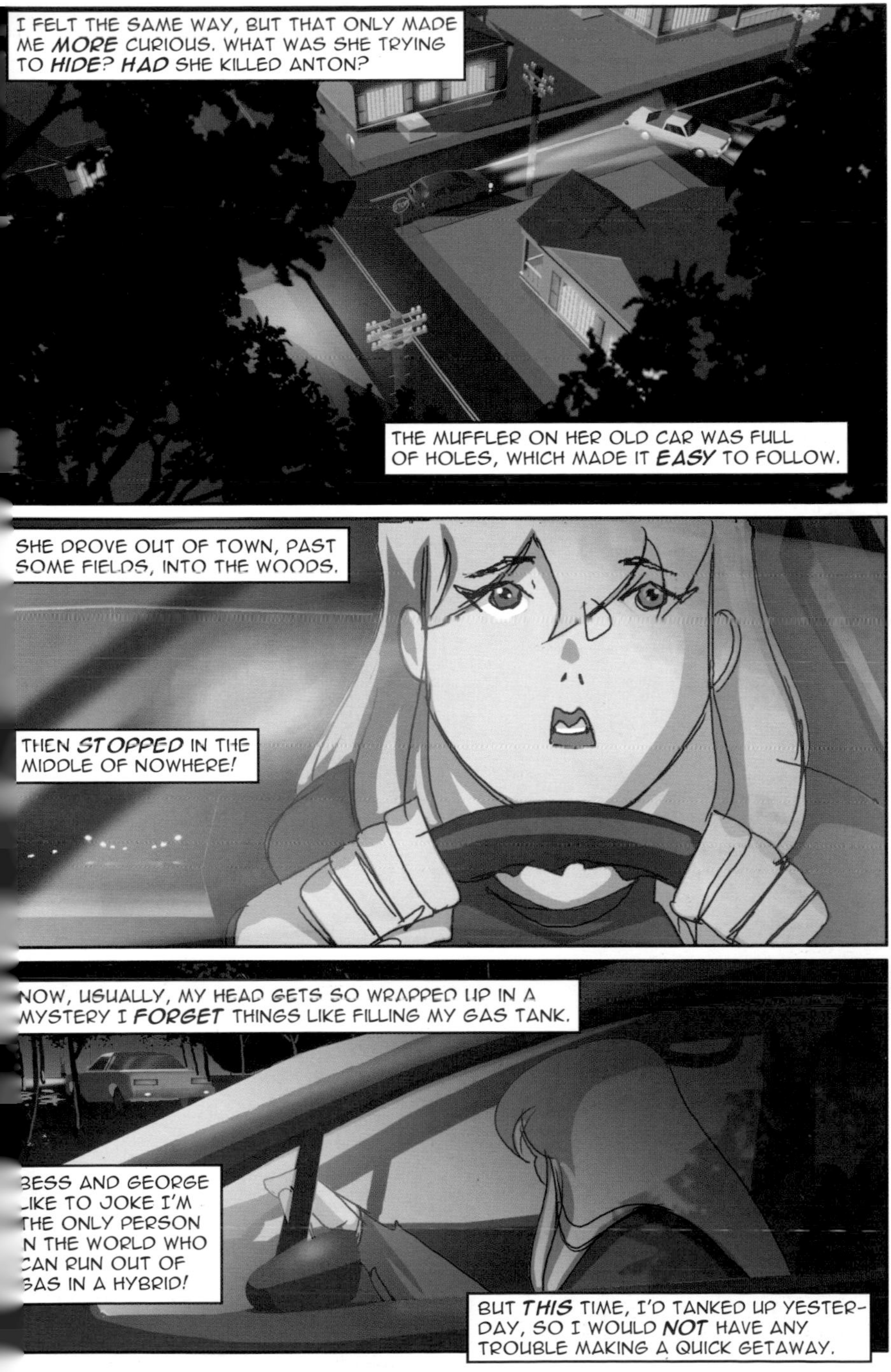
I FELT THE SAME WAY, BUT THAT ONLY MADE ME MORE CURIOUS. WHAT WAS SHE TRYING TO HIDE? HAD SHE KILLED ANTON?
THE MUFFLER ON HER OLD CAR WAS FULL OF HOLES, WHICH MADE IT EASY TO FOLLOW.
SHE DROVE OUT OF TOWN, PAST SOME FIELDS, INTO THE WOODS.
THEN STOPPED IN THE MIDDLE OF NOWHERE!
NOW, USUALLY, MY HEAD GETS SO WRAPPED UP IN A MYSTERY I FORGET THINGS LIKE FILLING MY GAS TANK.
BESS AND GEORGE LIKE TO JOKE I'M THE ONLY PERSON IN THE WORLD WHO CAN RUN OUT OF GAS IN A HYBRID!
BUT THIS TIME, I'D TANKED UP YESTERDAY, SO I WOULD NOT HAVE ANY TROUBLE MAKING A QUICK GETAWAY.

NOT SO MY DIGITAL *CAMERA*. IT'S IMPORTANT TO HAVE THAT SORT OF THING AROUND IF YOU WANT TO DO DETECTIVE WORK.

YOU NEVER KNOW WHEN YOU'LL NEED TO COLLECT *EVIDENCE*.

WHRRRRR

IT MADE A LITTLE WHIRRING SOUND AS IT POWERED UP, BUT I DON'T THINK MRS. DRUTHERS HEARD IT.

NOW I HAD HER!

CLICK

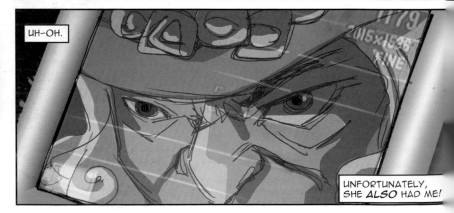

UH-OH.

UNFORTUNATELY, SHE *ALSO* HAD ME!

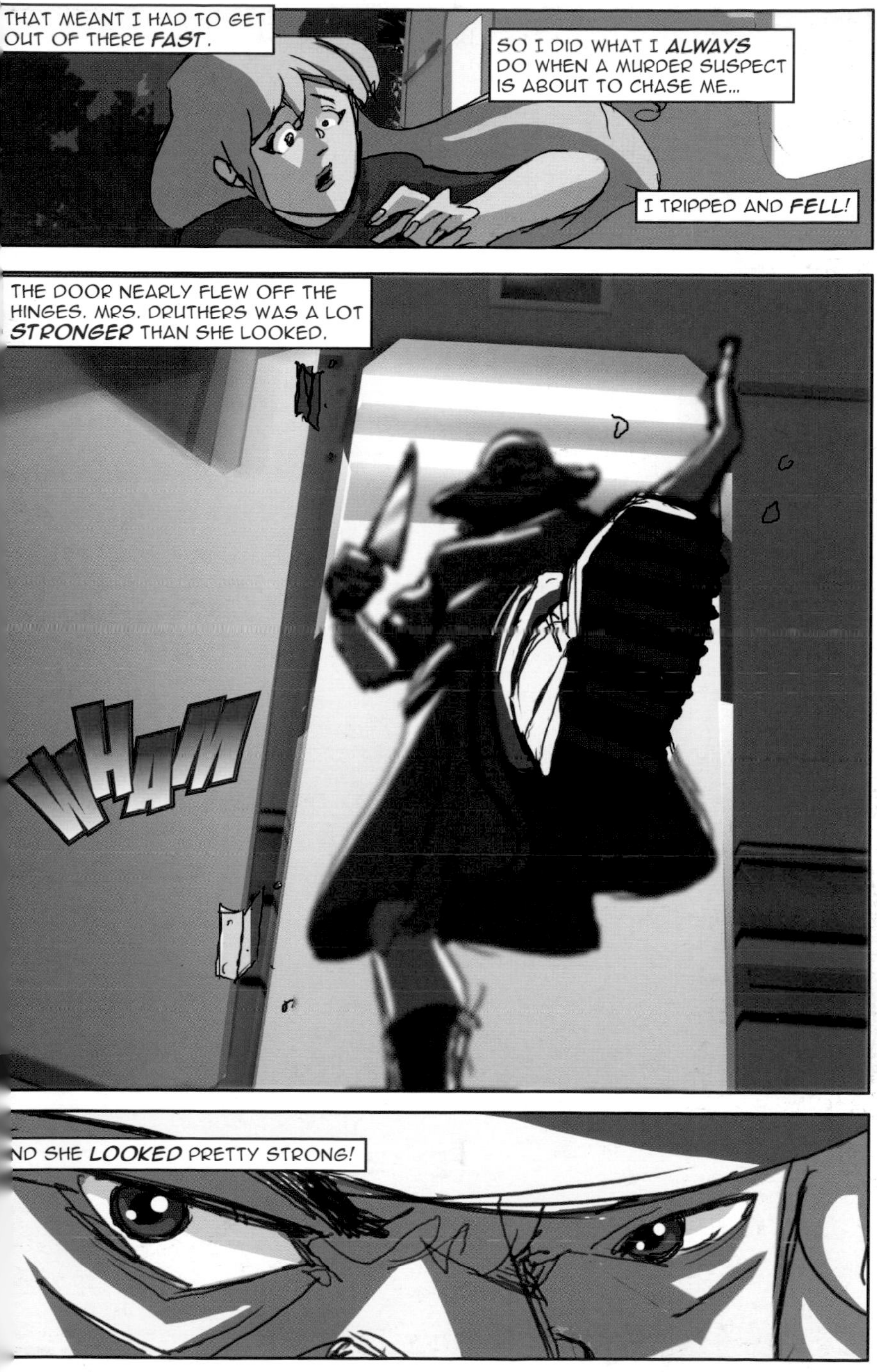
THAT MEANT I HAD TO GET OUT OF THERE FAST.
SO I DID WHAT I ALWAYS DO WHEN A MURDER SUSPECT IS ABOUT TO CHASE ME...
I TRIPPED AND FELL!
THE DOOR NEARLY FLEW OFF THE HINGES. MRS. DRUTHERS WAS A LOT STRONGER THAN SHE LOOKED.
WHAM
ND SHE LOOKED PRETTY STRONG!

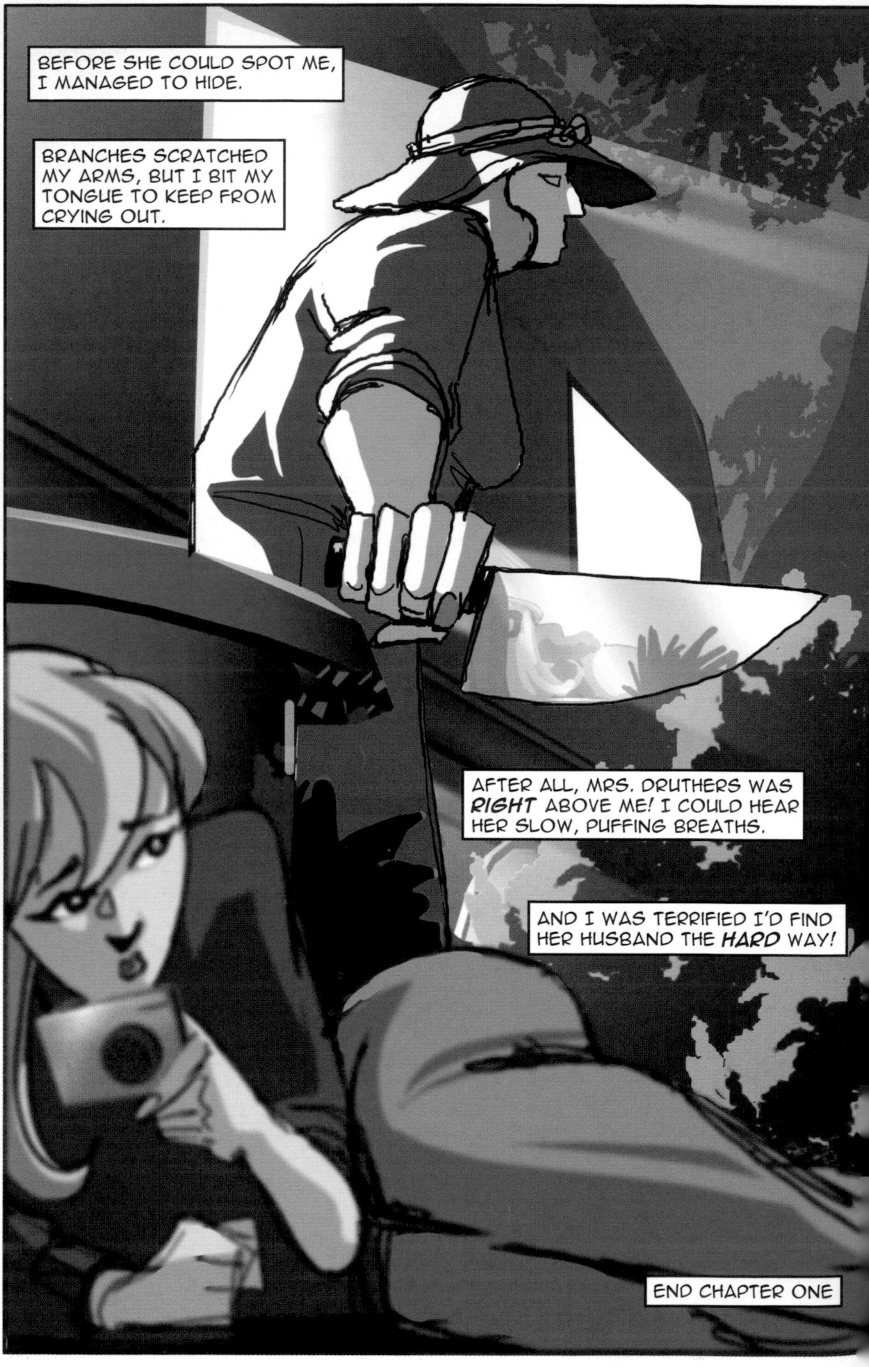

BEFORE SHE COULD SPOT ME, I MANAGED TO HIDE.
BRANCHES SCRATCHED MY ARMS, BUT I BIT MY TONGUE TO KEEP FROM CRYING OUT.
AFTER ALL, MRS. DRUTHERS WAS **RIGHT** ABOVE ME! I COULD HEAR HER SLOW, PUFFING BREATHS.
AND I WAS TERRIFIED I'D FIND HER HUSBAND THE **HARD** WAY!
END CHAPTER ONE

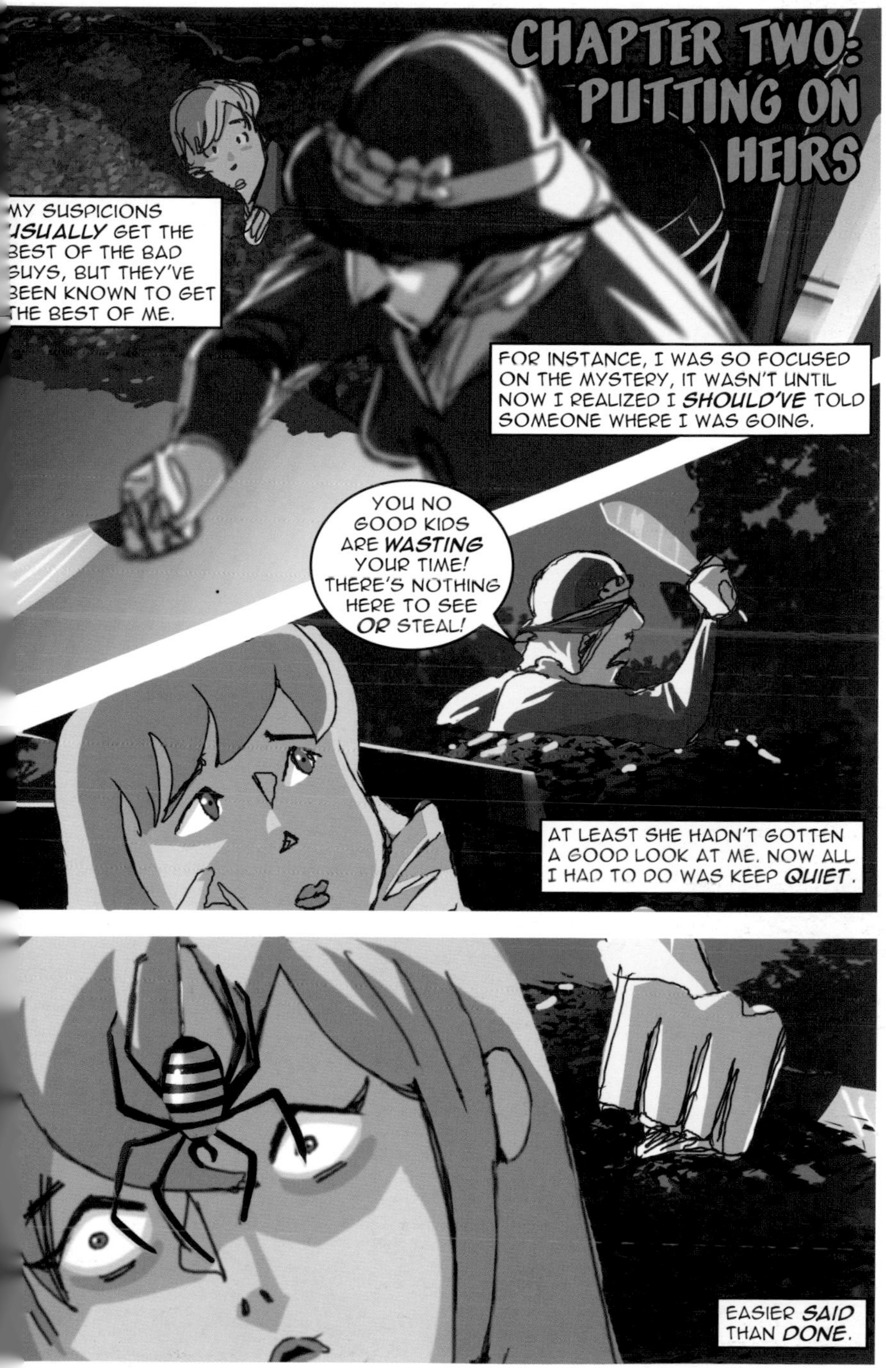
CHAPTER TWO: PUTTING ON HEIRS
MY SUSPICIONS USUALLY GET THE BEST OF THE BAD GUYS, BUT THEY'VE BEEN KNOWN TO GET THE BEST OF ME.
FOR INSTANCE, I WAS SO FOCUSED ON THE MYSTERY, IT WASN'T UNTIL NOW I REALIZED I SHOULD'VE TOLD SOMEONE WHERE I WAS GOING.
YOU NO GOOD KIDS ARE WASTING YOUR TIME! THERE'S NOTHING HERE TO SEE OR STEAL!
AT LEAST SHE HADN'T GOTTEN A GOOD LOOK AT ME. NOW ALL I HAD TO DO WAS KEEP QUIET.
EASIER SAID THAN DONE.

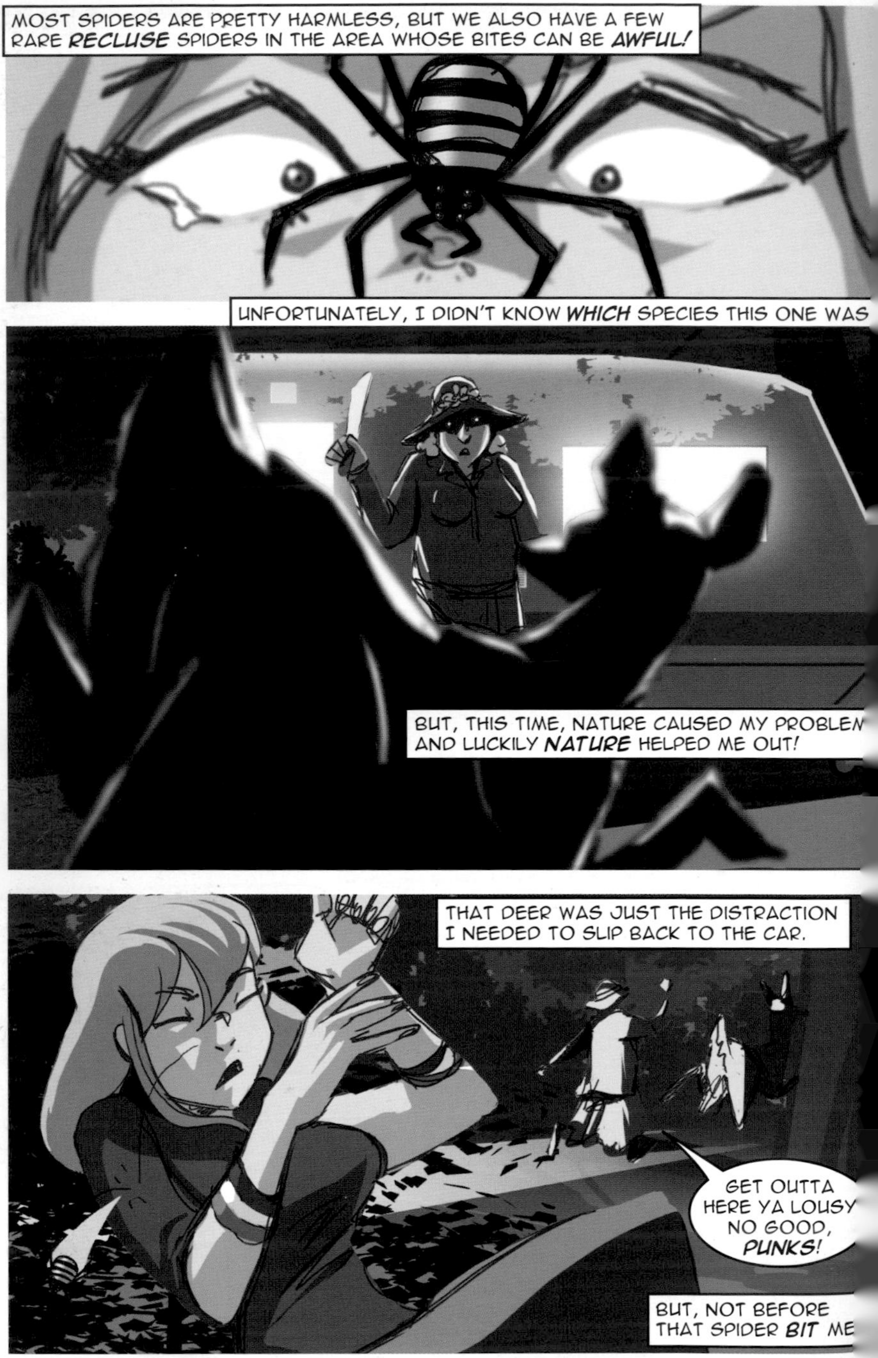

MOST SPIDERS ARE PRETTY HARMLESS, BUT WE ALSO HAVE A FEW RARE RECLUSE SPIDERS IN THE AREA WHOSE BITES CAN BE AWFUL!
UNFORTUNATELY, I DIDN'T KNOW WHICH SPECIES THIS ONE WAS
BUT, THIS TIME, NATURE CAUSED MY PROBLEM AND LUCKILY NATURE HELPED ME OUT!
THAT DEER WAS JUST THE DISTRACTION I NEEDED TO SLIP BACK TO THE CAR.
GET OUTTA HERE YA LOUSY NO GOOD, PUNKS!
BUT, NOT BEFORE THAT SPIDER BIT ME

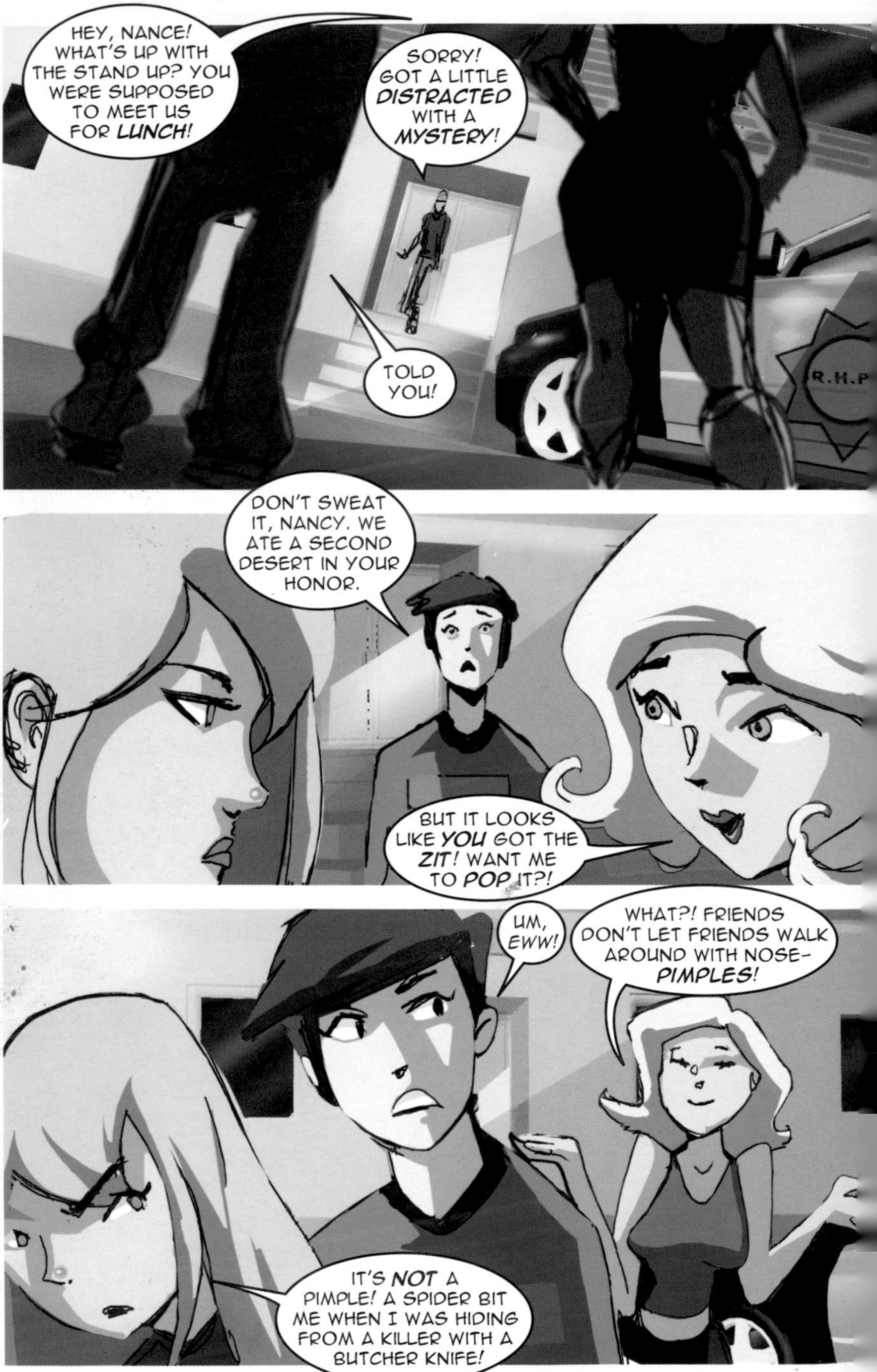
HEY, NANCE! WHAT'S UP WITH THE STAND UP? YOU WERE SUPPOSED TO MEET US FOR *LUNCH*!
SORRY! GOT A LITTLE *DISTRACTED* WITH A *MYSTERY*!
TOLD YOU!
DON'T SWEAT IT, NANCY. WE ATE A SECOND DESERT IN YOUR HONOR.
BUT IT LOOKS LIKE *YOU* GOT THE *ZIT*! WANT ME TO *POP* IT?!
UM, EWW!
WHAT?! FRIENDS DON'T LET FRIENDS WALK AROUND WITH NOSE-*PIMPLES*!
IT'S *NOT* A PIMPLE! A SPIDER BIT ME WHEN I WAS HIDING FROM A KILLER WITH A BUTCHER KNIFE!

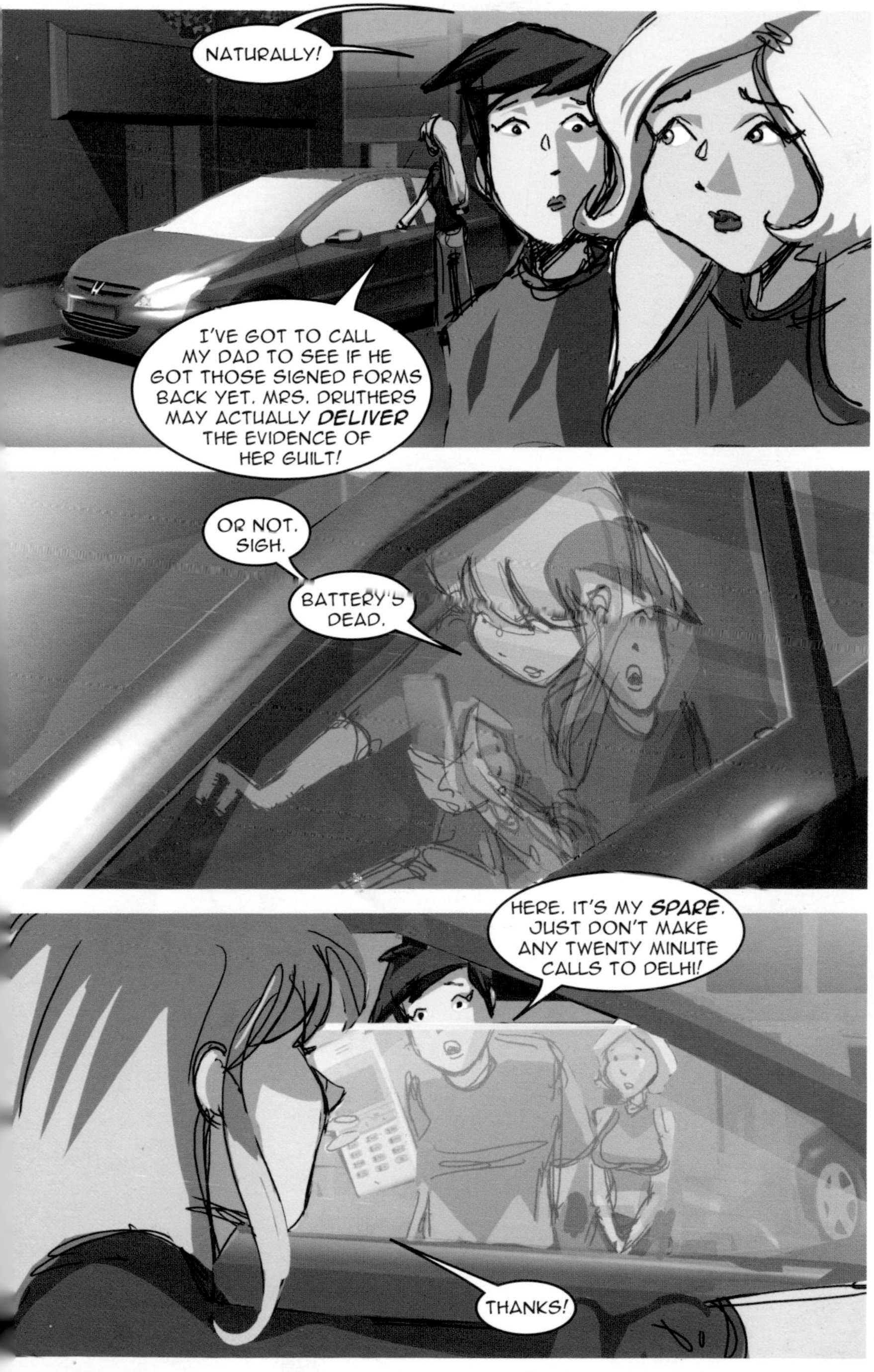
NATURALLY!
I'VE GOT TO CALL MY DAD TO SEE IF HE GOT THOSE SIGNED FORMS BACK YET. MRS. DRUTHERS MAY ACTUALLY *DELIVER* THE EVIDENCE OF HER GUILT!
OR NOT. SIGH.
BATTERY'S DEAD.
HERE. IT'S MY *SPARE*. JUST DON'T MAKE ANY TWENTY MINUTE CALLS TO DELHI!
THANKS!

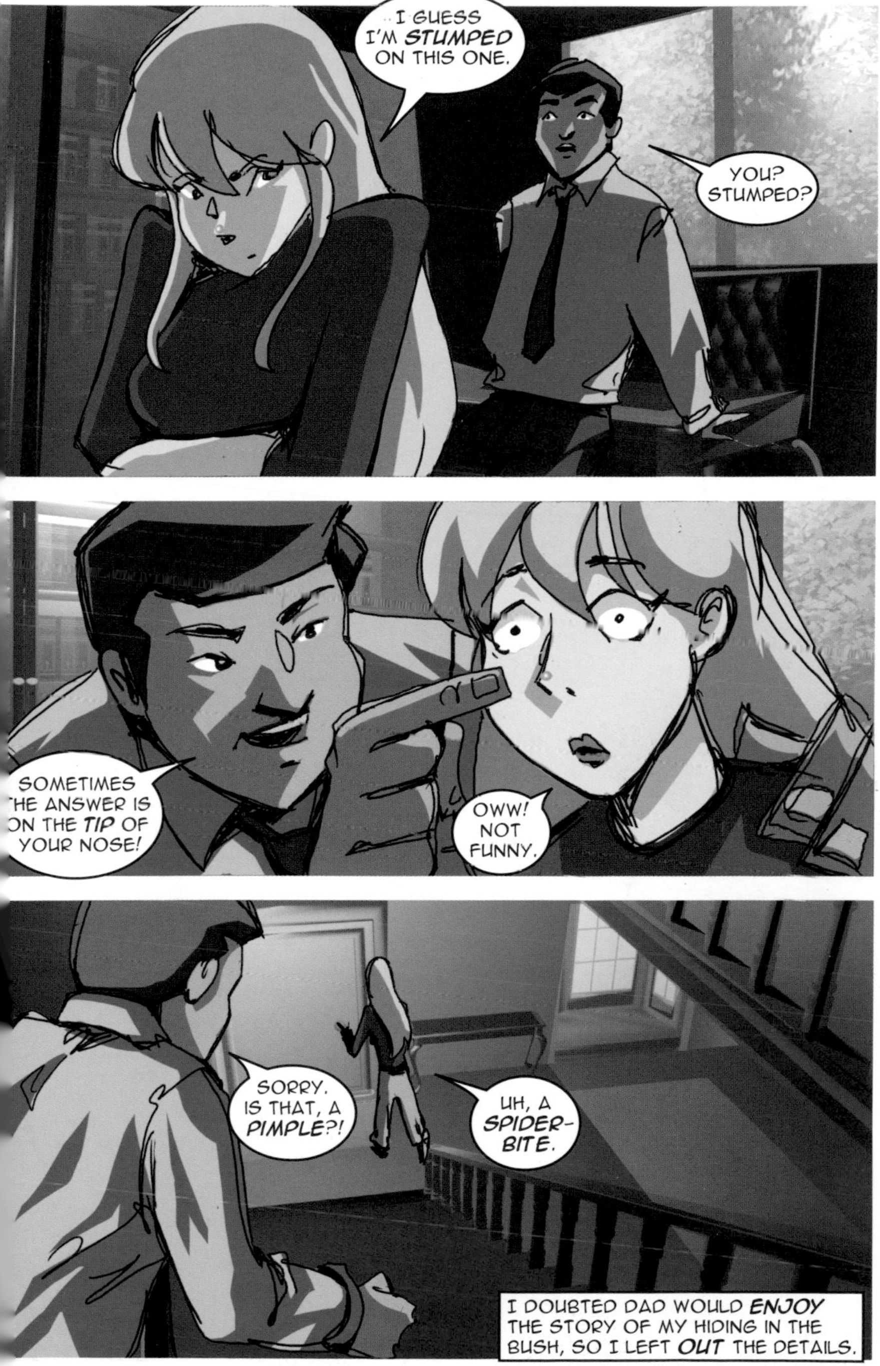
..I GUESS I'M STUMPED ON THIS ONE.
YOU? STUMPED?
SOMETIMES THE ANSWER IS ON THE TIP OF YOUR NOSE!
OWW! NOT FUNNY.
SORRY. IS THAT, A PIMPLE?!
UH, A SPIDER-BITE.
I DOUBTED DAD WOULD ENJOY THE STORY OF MY HIDING IN THE BUSH, SO I LEFT OUT THE DETAILS.

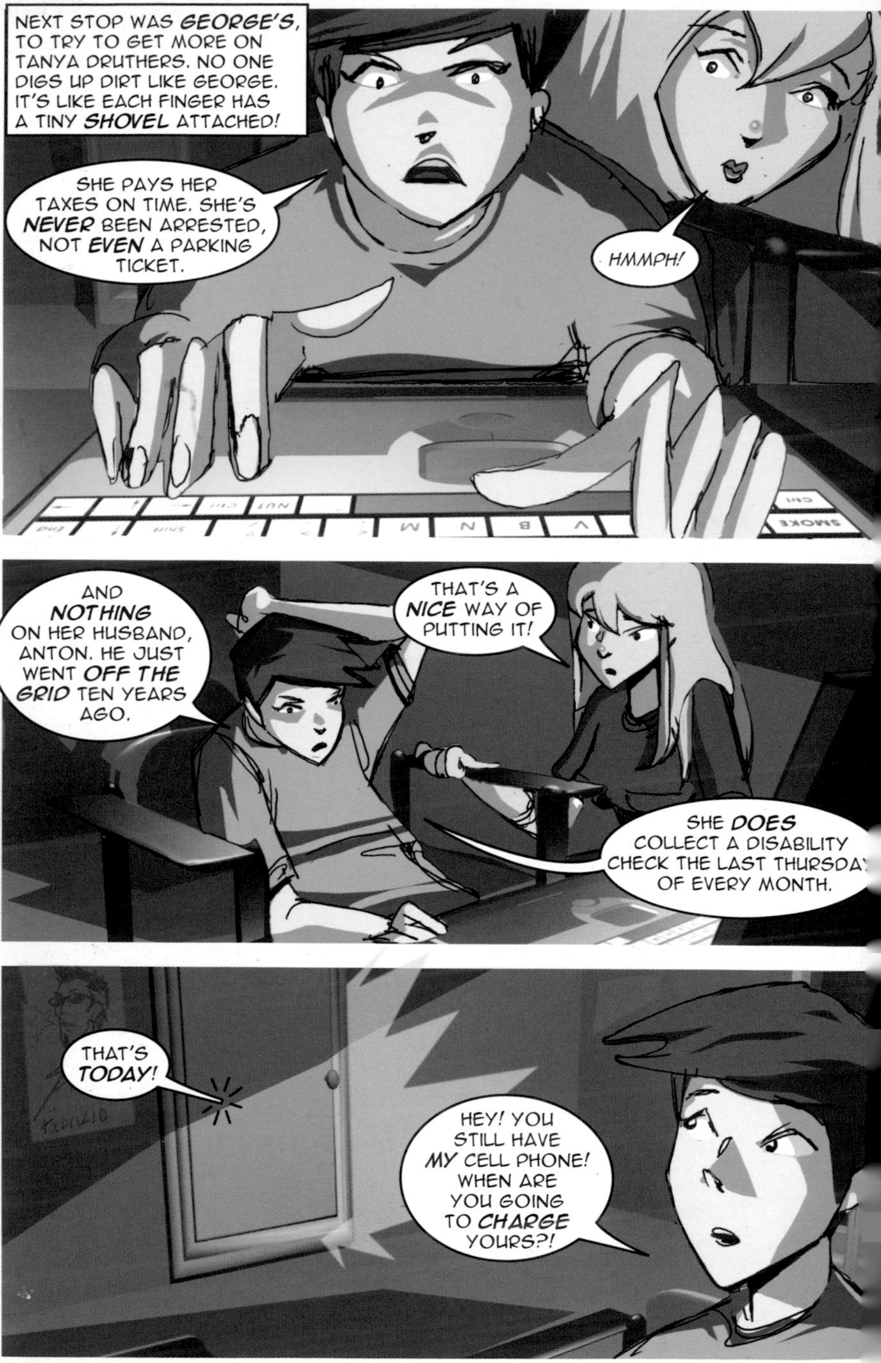
NEXT STOP WAS GEORGE'S, TO TRY TO GET MORE ON TANYA DRUTHERS. NO ONE DIGS UP DIRT LIKE GEORGE. IT'S LIKE EACH FINGER HAS A TINY SHOVEL ATTACHED!
SHE PAYS HER TAXES ON TIME. SHE'S NEVER BEEN ARRESTED, NOT EVEN A PARKING TICKET.
HMMPH!
AND NOTHING ON HER HUSBAND, ANTON. HE JUST WENT OFF THE GRID TEN YEARS AGO.
THAT'S A NICE WAY OF PUTTING IT!
SHE DOES COLLECT A DISABILITY CHECK THE LAST THURSDA OF EVERY MONTH.
THAT'S TODAY!
HEY! YOU STILL HAVE MY CELL PHONE! WHEN ARE YOU GOING TO CHARGE YOURS?!

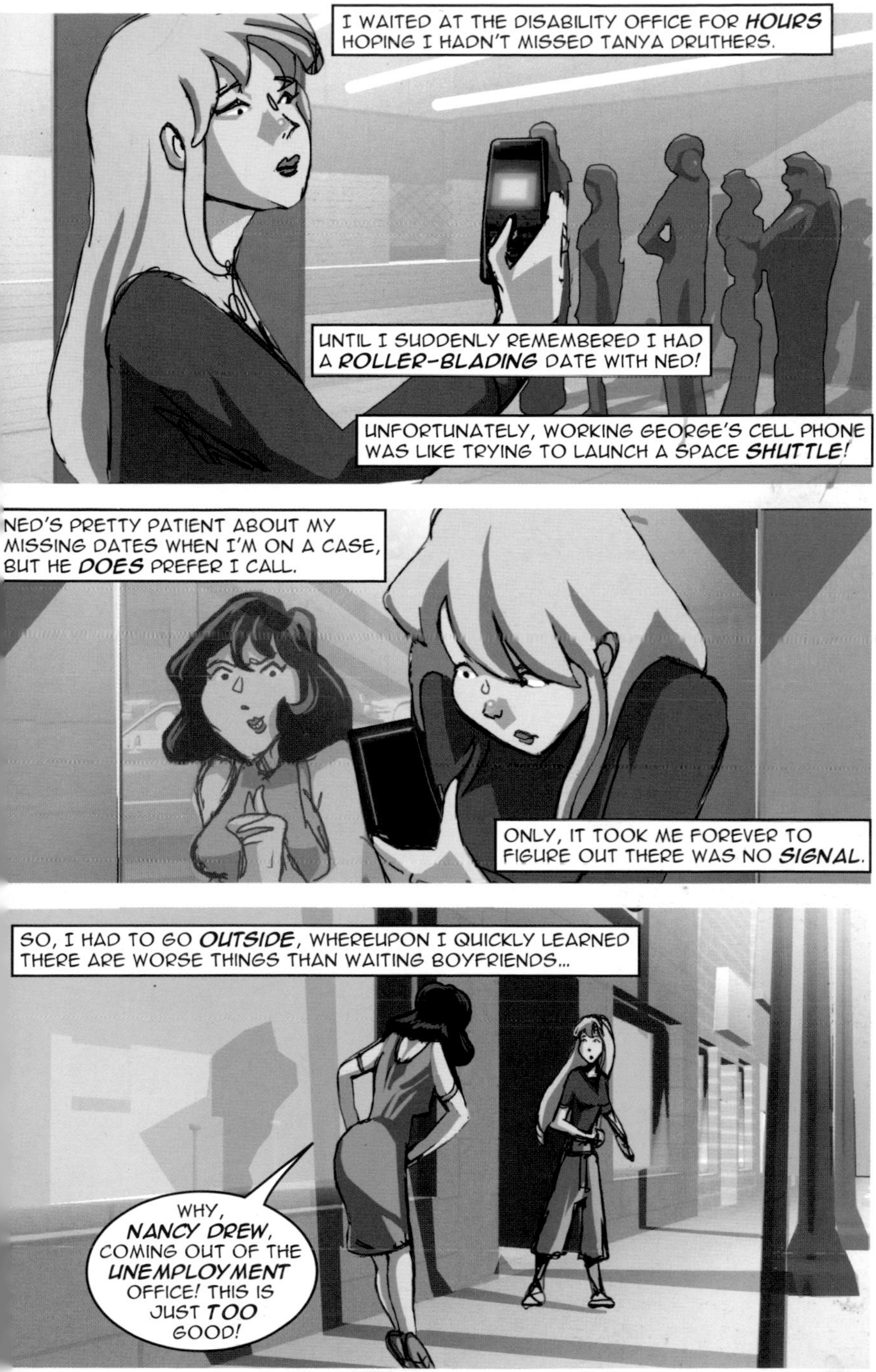
I WAITED AT THE DISABILITY OFFICE FOR HOURS HOPING I HADN'T MISSED TANYA DRUTHERS.
UNTIL I SUDDENLY REMEMBERED I HAD A ROLLER-BLADING DATE WITH NED!
UNFORTUNATELY, WORKING GEORGE'S CELL PHONE WAS LIKE TRYING TO LAUNCH A SPACE SHUTTLE!
NED'S PRETTY PATIENT ABOUT MY MISSING DATES WHEN I'M ON A CASE, BUT HE DOES PREFER I CALL.
ONLY, IT TOOK ME FOREVER TO FIGURE OUT THERE WAS NO SIGNAL.
SO, I HAD TO GO OUTSIDE, WHEREUPON I QUICKLY LEARNED THERE ARE WORSE THINGS THAN WAITING BOYFRIENDS...
WHY, NANCY DREW, COMING OUT OF THE UNEMPLOYMENT OFFICE! THIS IS JUST TOO GOOD!

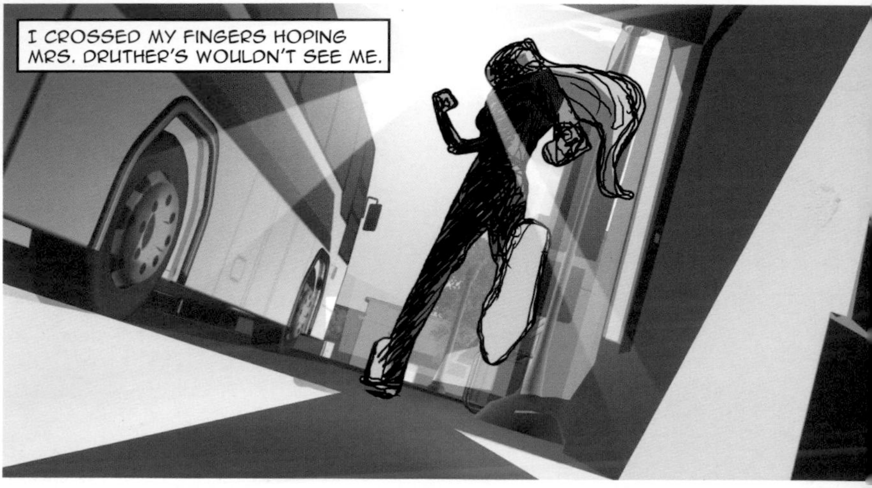
I CROSSED MY FINGERS HOPING MRS. DRUTHER'S WOULDN'T SEE ME.

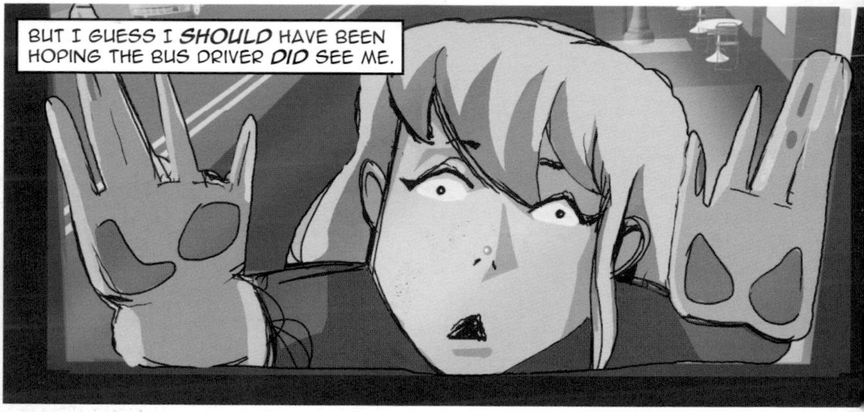
BUT I GUESS I *SHOULD* HAVE BEEN HOPING THE BUS DRIVER *DID* SEE ME.

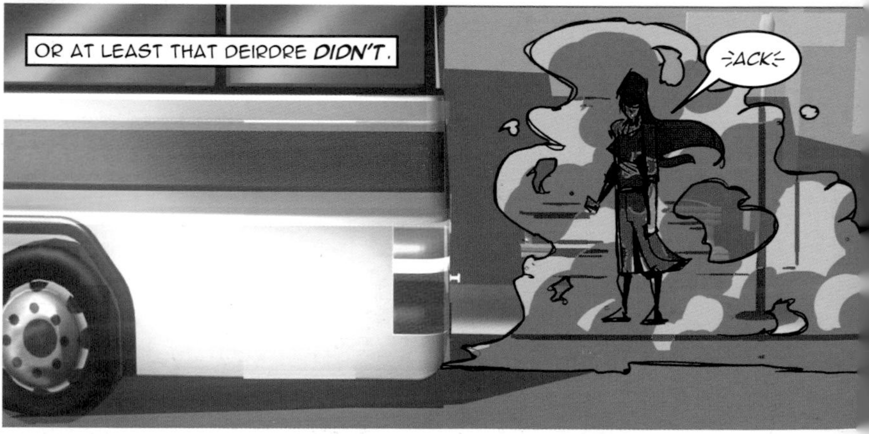
OR AT LEAST THAT DEIRDRE *DIDN'T*.
=ACK=

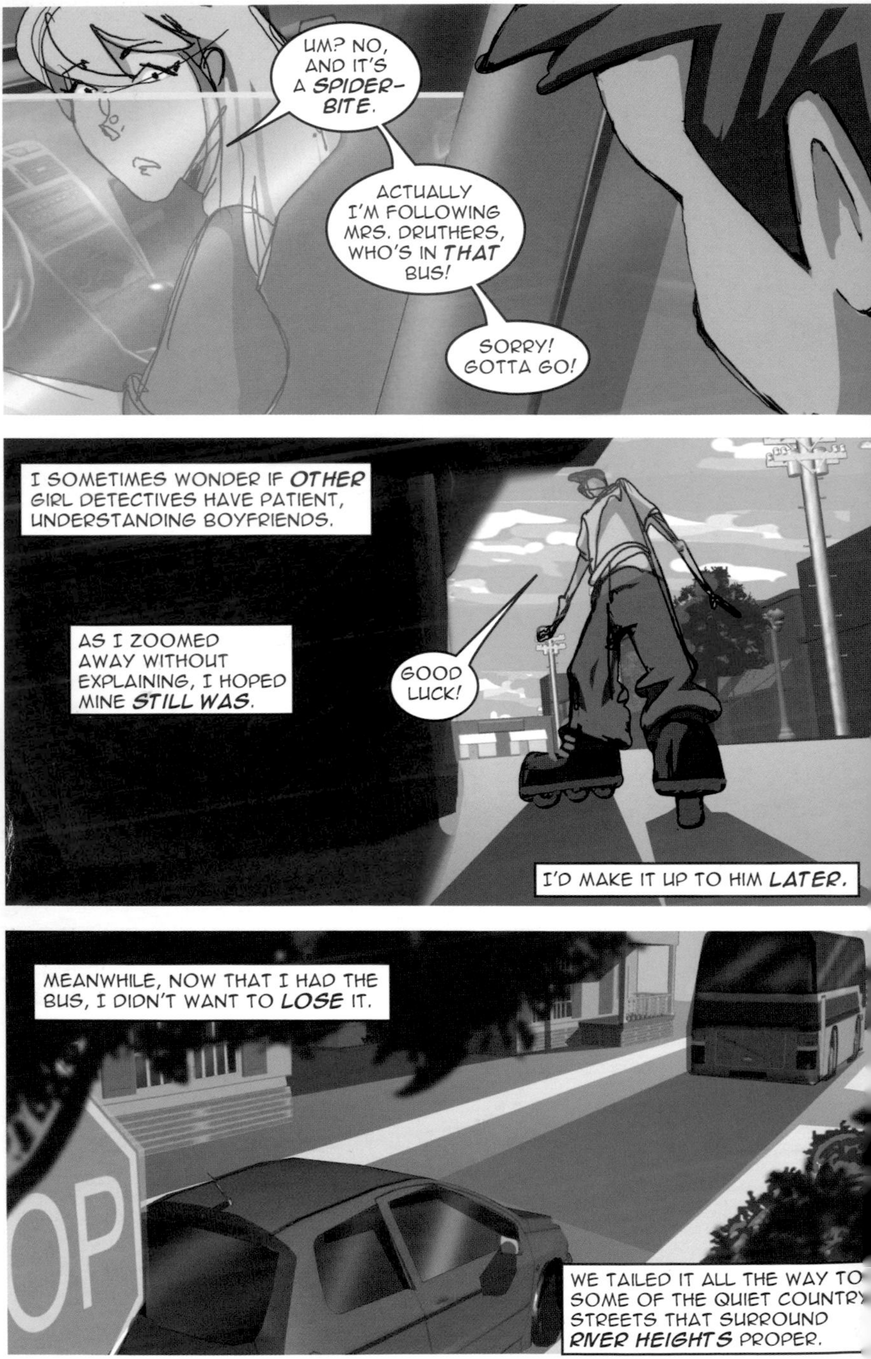
UM? NO, AND IT'S A SPIDER-BITE.
ACTUALLY I'M FOLLOWING MRS. DRUTHERS, WHO'S IN THAT BUS!
SORRY! GOTTA GO!
I SOMETIMES WONDER IF OTHER GIRL DETECTIVES HAVE PATIENT, UNDERSTANDING BOYFRIENDS.
AS I ZOOMED AWAY WITHOUT EXPLAINING, I HOPED MINE STILL WAS.
GOOD LUCK!
I'D MAKE IT UP TO HIM LATER.
MEANWHILE, NOW THAT I HAD THE BUS, I DIDN'T WANT TO LOSE IT.
WE TAILED IT ALL THE WAY TO SOME OF THE QUIET COUNTRY STREETS THAT SURROUND RIVER HEIGHTS PROPER.

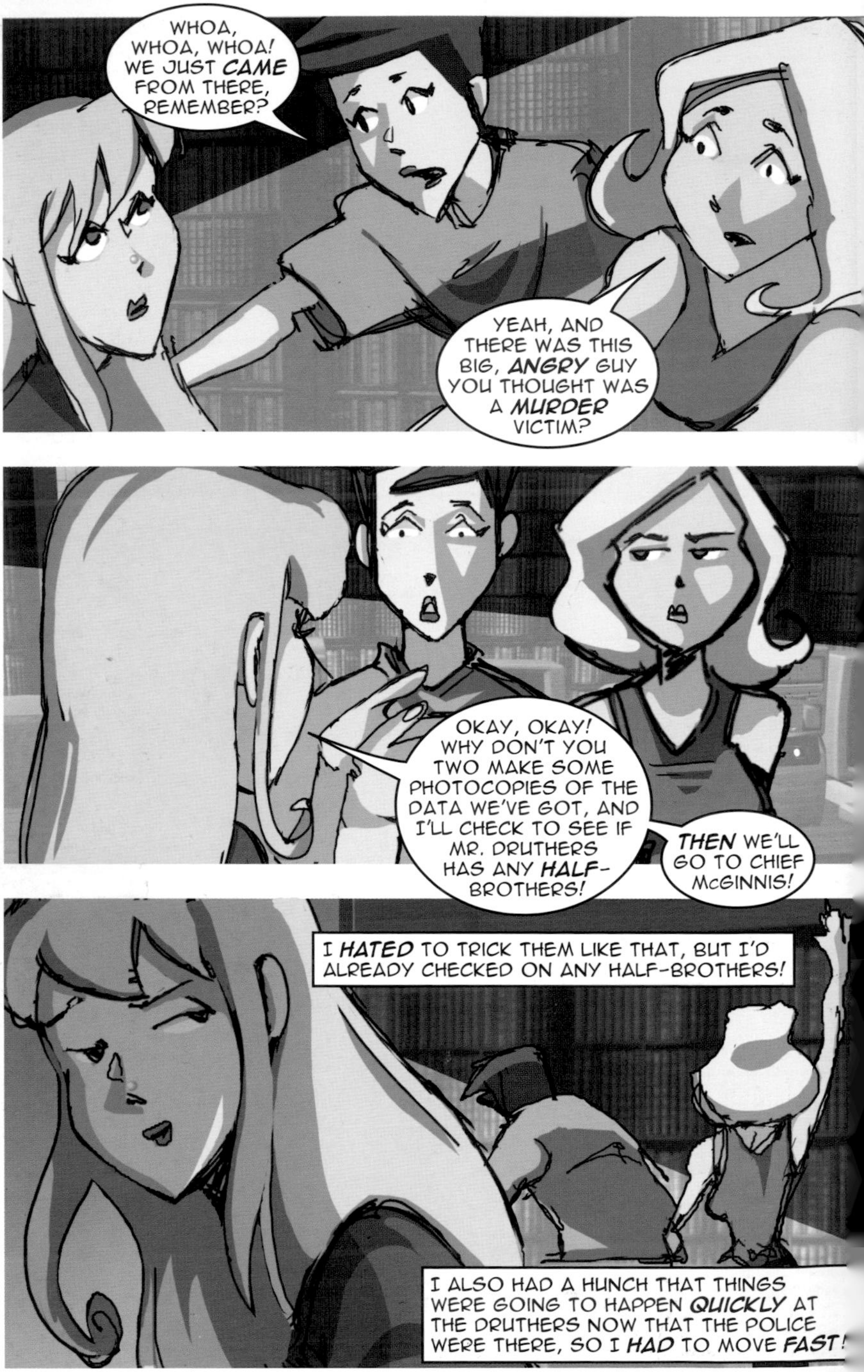
WHOA, WHOA, WHOA! WE JUST CAME FROM THERE, REMEMBER?
YEAH, AND THERE WAS THIS BIG, ANGRY GUY YOU THOUGHT WAS A MURDER VICTIM?
OKAY, OKAY! WHY DON'T YOU TWO MAKE SOME PHOTOCOPIES OF THE DATA WE'VE GOT, AND I'LL CHECK TO SEE IF MR. DRUTHERS HAS ANY HALF-BROTHERS!
THEN WE'LL GO TO CHIEF McGINNIS!
I HATED TO TRICK THEM LIKE THAT, BUT I'D ALREADY CHECKED ON ANY HALF-BROTHERS!
I ALSO HAD A HUNCH THAT THINGS WERE GOING TO HAPPEN QUICKLY AT THE DRUTHERS NOW THAT THE POLICE WERE THERE, SO I HAD TO MOVE FAST!

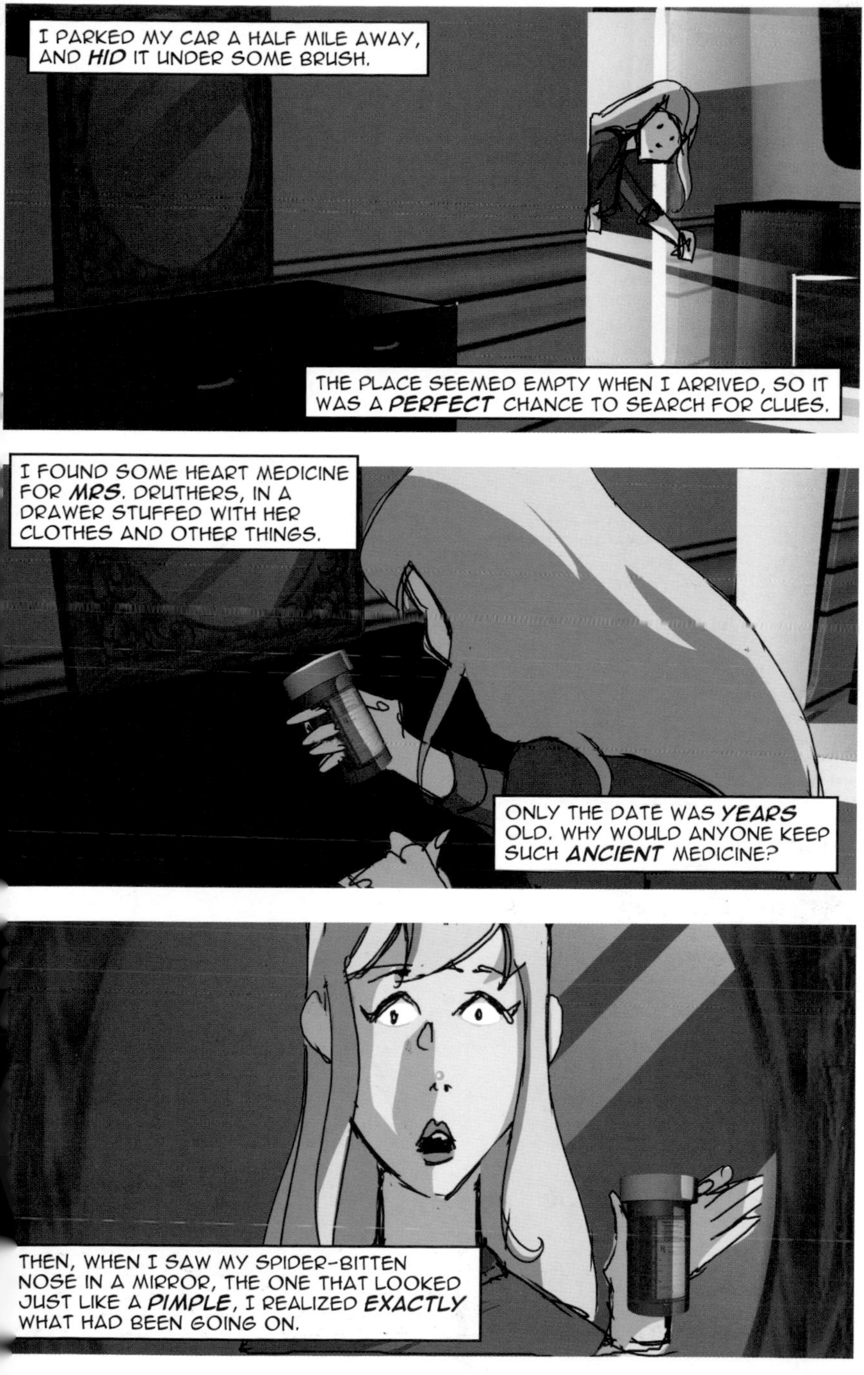
I PARKED MY CAR A HALF MILE AWAY, AND *HID* IT UNDER SOME BRUSH.
THE PLACE SEEMED EMPTY WHEN I ARRIVED, SO IT WAS A *PERFECT* CHANCE TO SEARCH FOR CLUES.
I FOUND SOME HEART MEDICINE FOR *MRS*. DRUTHERS, IN A DRAWER STUFFED WITH HER CLOTHES AND OTHER THINGS.
ONLY THE DATE WAS *YEARS* OLD. WHY WOULD ANYONE KEEP SUCH *ANCIENT* MEDICINE?
THEN, WHEN I SAW MY SPIDER-BITTEN NOSE IN A MIRROR, THE ONE THAT LOOKED JUST LIKE A *PIMPLE*, I REALIZED *EXACTLY* WHAT HAD BEEN GOING ON.

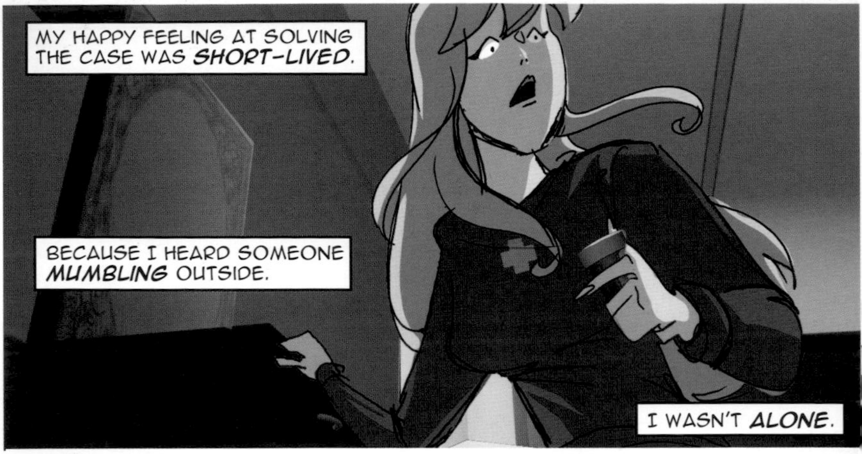
MY HAPPY FEELING AT SOLVING THE CASE WAS *SHORT-LIVED*.
BECAUSE I HEARD SOMEONE *MUMBLING* OUTSIDE.
I WASN'T *ALONE*.

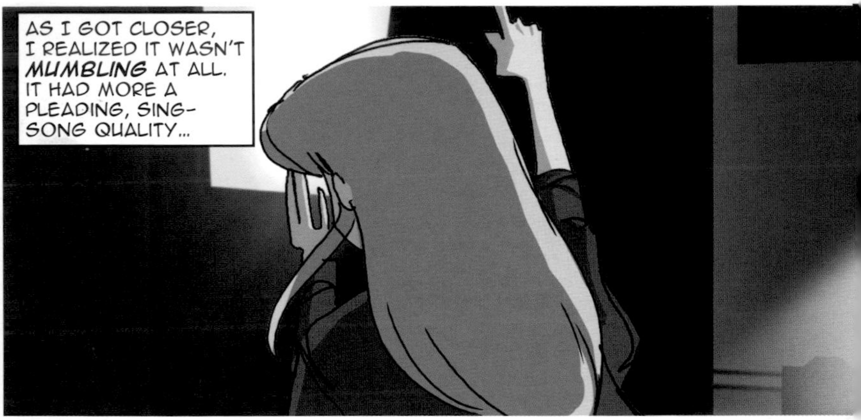
AS I GOT CLOSER, I REALIZED IT WASN'T *MUMBLING* AT ALL. IT HAD MORE A PLEADING, SING-SONG QUALITY...

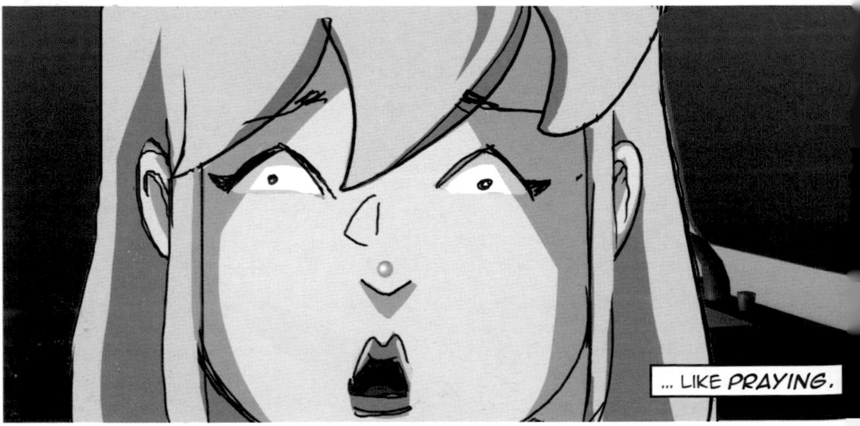
... LIKE *PRAYING*.

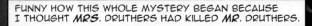

FUNNY HOW THIS WHOLE MYSTERY BEGAN BECAUSE I THOUGHT *MRS.* DRUTHERS HAD KILLED *MR.* DRUTHERS.

NOW IT LOOKED A LOT MORE LIKE *HE'D* KILLED *HER!*

THAT'S ANOTHER THING ABOUT DETECTIVE WORK, YOU CAN *NEVER* BE *TOO* QUIET.

CRACK

EH?

YOU! *AGAIN!*

ULP! SORRY? AGAIN?

Y'KNOW, YOU THINK I'D BE USED TO THIS SORT OF THING BY NOW.
I MEAN, I HIDE A LOT DURING MY CASES. USUALLY, I DON'T GET CAUGHT, BUT HEY, SOMETIMES I DO.
SO, YOU'D THINK I'D BE PREPARED, THAT AT LEAST MY HEART WOULDN'T LEAP INTO MY THROAT WITH FEAR, OR MY KNEES WOULDN'T SHAKE SO MUCH.
BUT, I GUESS SOME THINGS, NO MATTER HOW OFTEN THEY HAPPEN, STILL FEEL LIKE THE FIRST TIME!

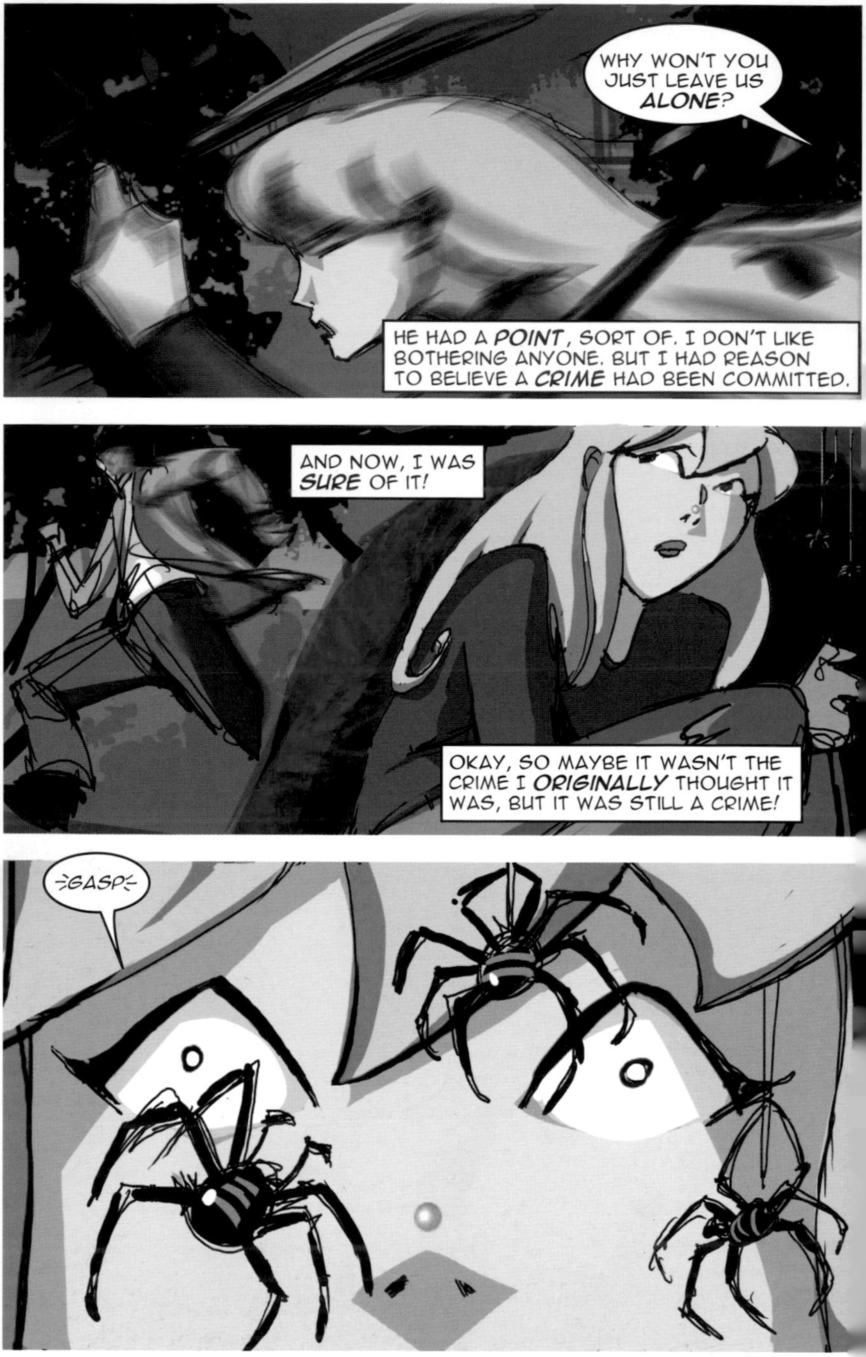

WHY WON'T YOU JUST LEAVE US ALONE?
HE HAD A POINT, SORT OF. I DON'T LIKE BOTHERING ANYONE. BUT I HAD REASON TO BELIEVE A CRIME HAD BEEN COMMITTED.
AND NOW, I WAS SURE OF IT!
OKAY, SO MAYBE IT WASN'T THE CRIME I ORIGINALLY THOUGHT IT WAS, BUT IT WAS STILL A CRIME!
GASP

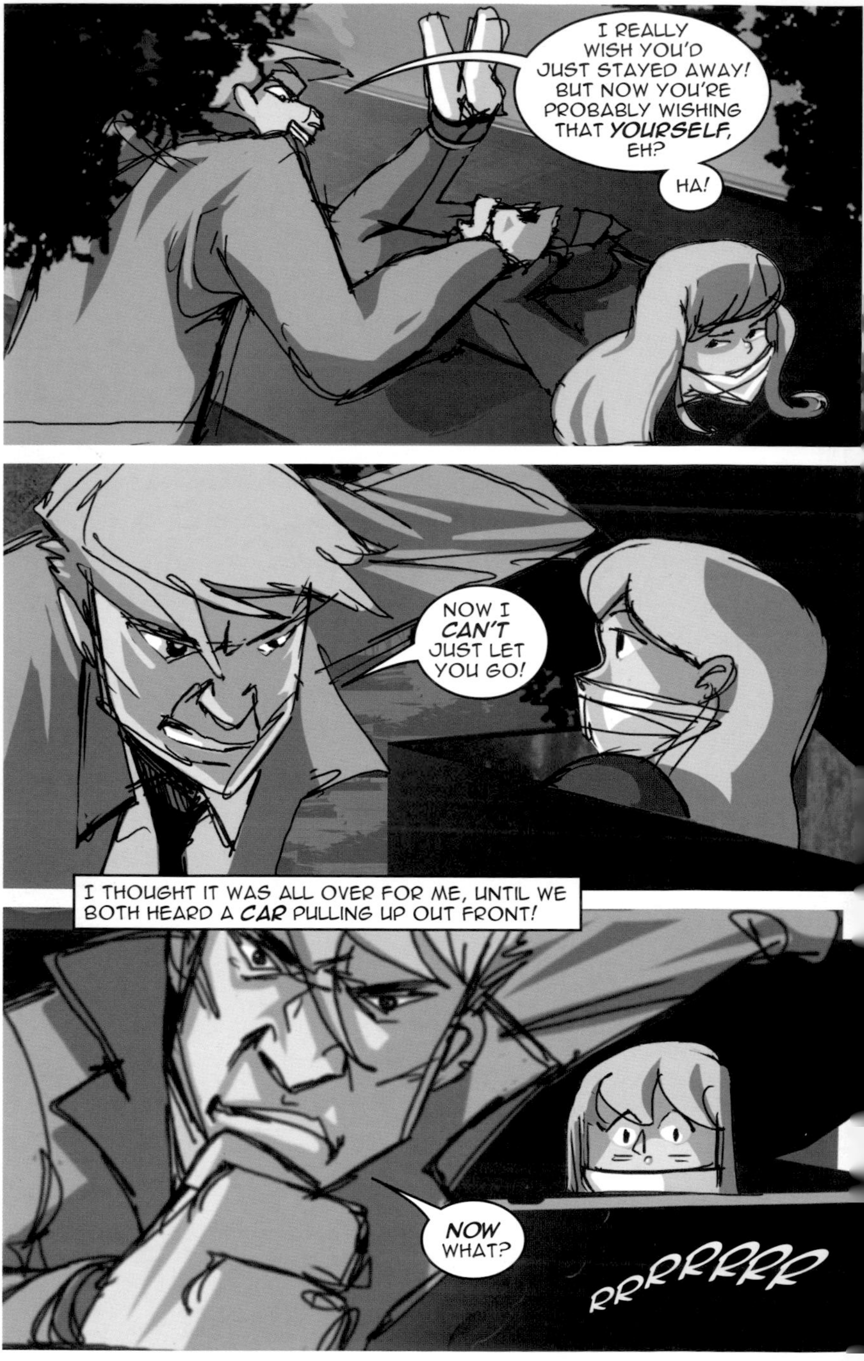
I REALLY WISH YOU'D JUST STAYED AWAY! BUT NOW YOU'RE PROBABLY WISHING THAT *YOURSELF*, EH?
HA!
NOW I *CAN'T* JUST LET YOU GO!
I THOUGHT IT WAS ALL OVER FOR ME, UNTIL WE BOTH HEARD A *CAR* PULLING UP OUT FRONT!
NOW WHAT?
RRRRRRRR

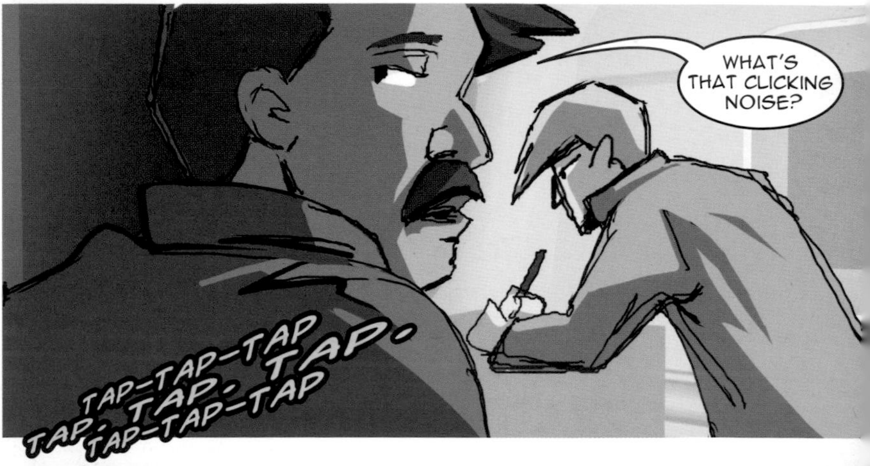
WHAT'S THAT CLICKING NOISE?
TAP-TAP-TAP TAP. TAP. TAP. TAP-TAP-TAP

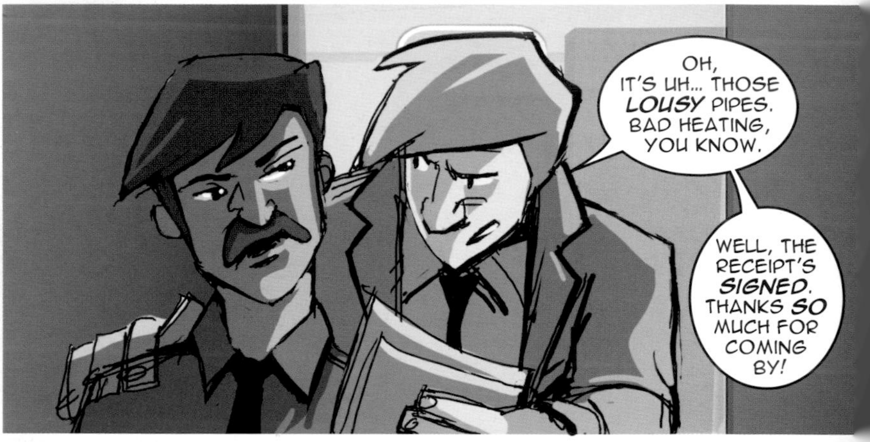
OH, IT'S UH... THOSE LOUSY PIPES. BAD HEATING, YOU KNOW.
WELL, THE RECEIPT'S SIGNED. THANKS SO MUCH FOR COMING BY!

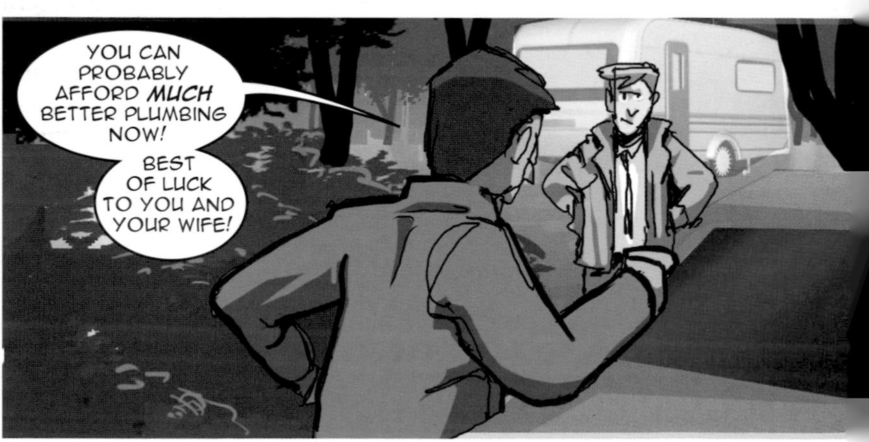
YOU CAN PROBABLY AFFORD MUCH BETTER PLUMBING NOW!
BEST OF LUCK TO YOU AND YOUR WIFE!

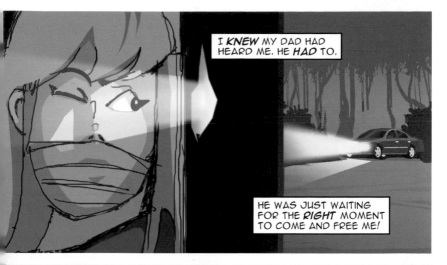

I *KNEW* MY DAD HAD HEARD ME. HE *HAD* TO.

HE WAS JUST WAITING FOR THE *RIGHT* MOMENT TO COME AND FREE ME!

AND... AND... HE WAS JUST SHAKING HANDS WITH MR. DRUTHERS TO *LULL* HIM INTO A FALSE SENSE OF SECURITY.

YEAH, *THAT* WAS IT.

ONLY THEN, HE *DROVE* AWAY!

WHICH MEANT ⇒*ULP*⇐ MAYBE HE *DIDN'T* GET THE MESSAGE!

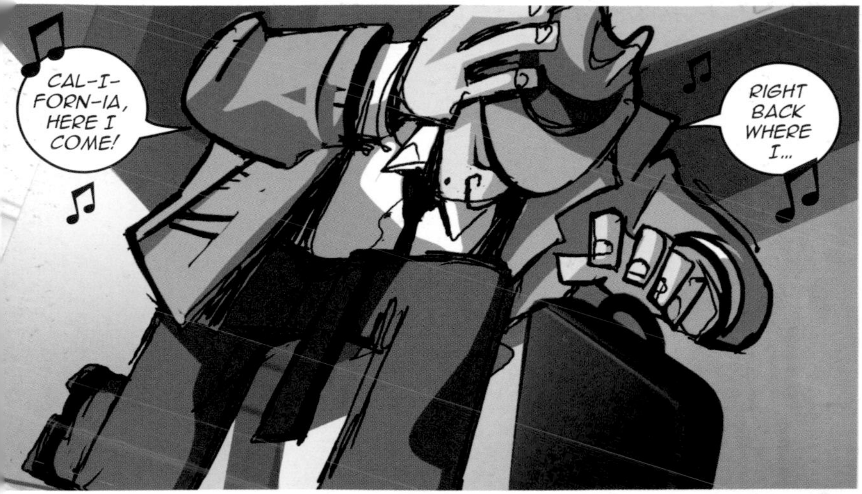
CAL-I-FORN-IA, HERE I COME!
RIGHT BACK WHERE I...

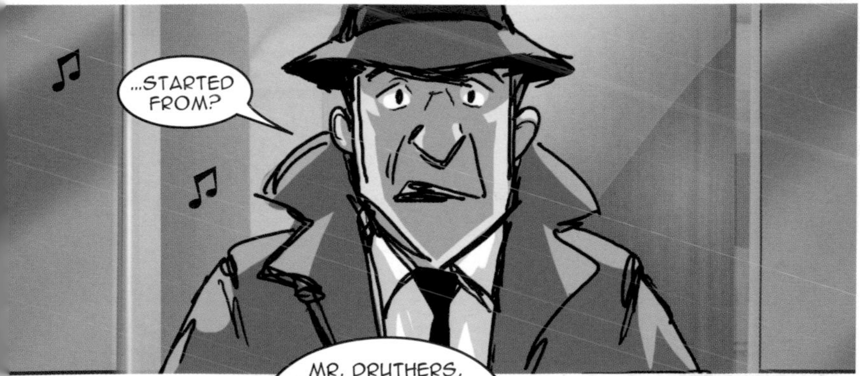
...STARTED FROM?

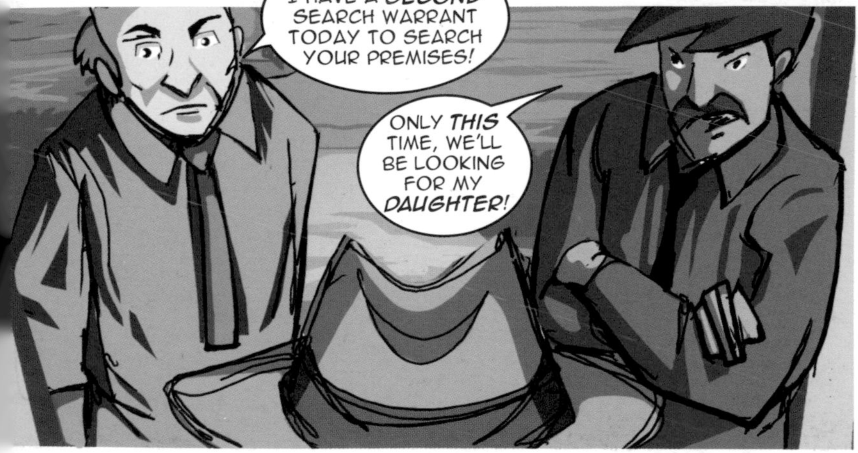
MR. DRUTHERS, I HAVE A SECOND SEARCH WARRANT TODAY TO SEARCH YOUR PREMISES!
ONLY THIS TIME, WE'LL BE LOOKING FOR MY DAUGHTER!

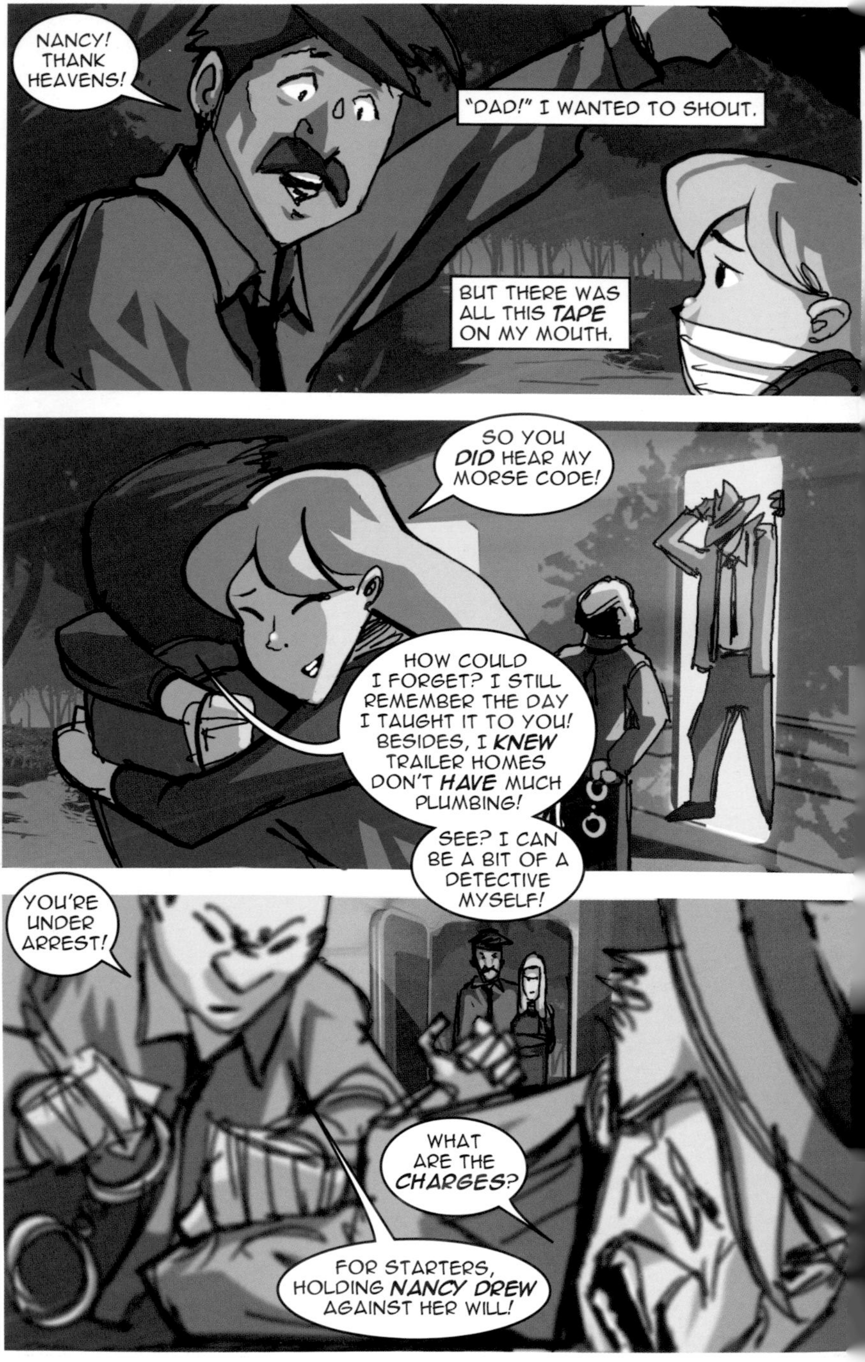
NANCY! THANK HEAVENS!
"DAD!" I WANTED TO SHOUT.
BUT THERE WAS ALL THIS TAPE ON MY MOUTH.
SO YOU DID HEAR MY MORSE CODE!
HOW COULD I FORGET? I STILL REMEMBER THE DAY I TAUGHT IT TO YOU! BESIDES, I KNEW TRAILER HOMES DON'T HAVE MUCH PLUMBING!
SEE? I CAN BE A BIT OF A DETECTIVE MYSELF!
YOU'RE UNDER ARREST!
WHAT ARE THE CHARGES?
FOR STARTERS, HOLDING NANCY DREW AGAINST HER WILL!

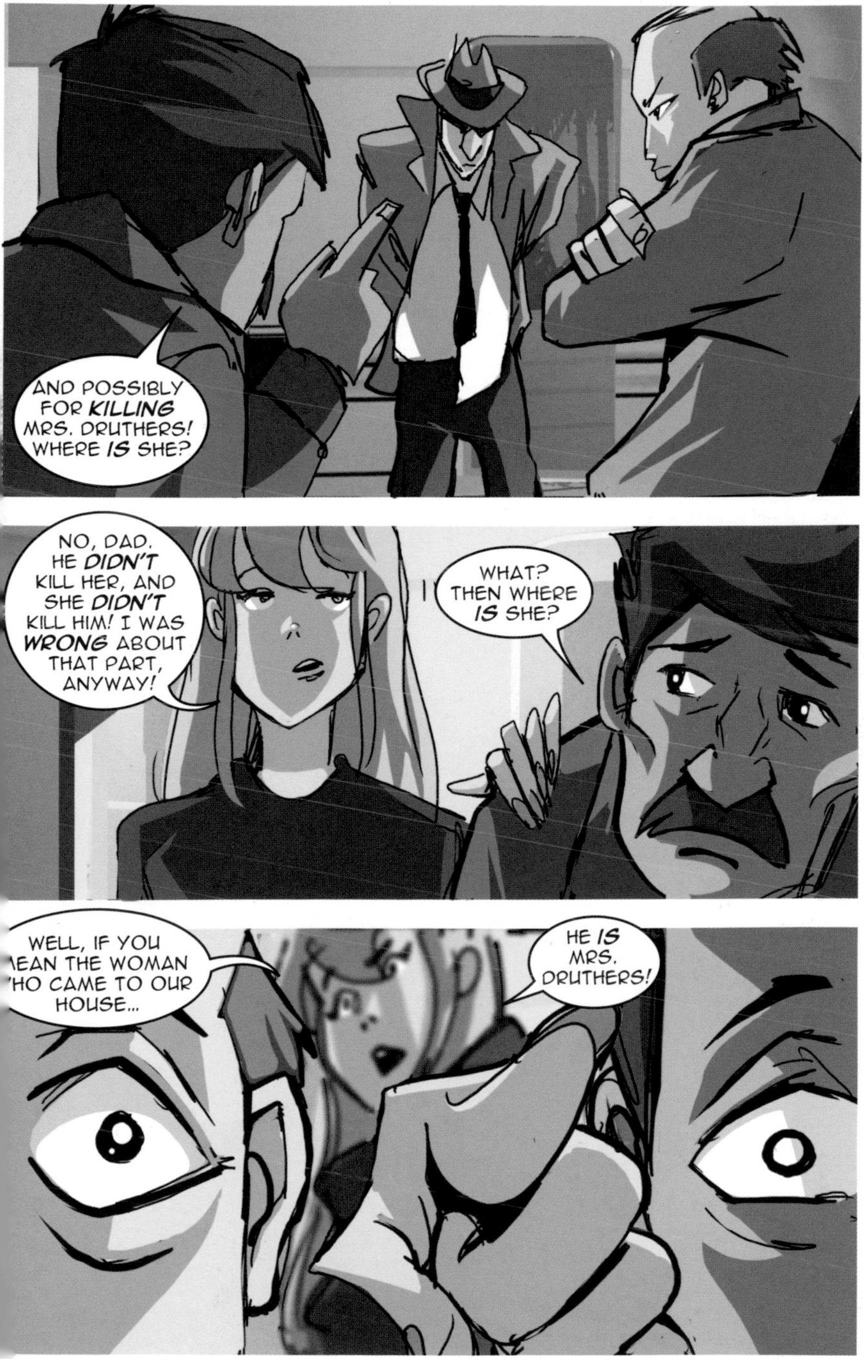
AND POSSIBLY FOR *KILLING* MRS. DRUTHERS! WHERE *IS* SHE?
NO, DAD. HE *DIDN'T* KILL HER, AND SHE *DIDN'T* KILL HIM! I WAS *WRONG* ABOUT THAT PART, ANYWAY!
WHAT? THEN WHERE *IS* SHE?
WELL, IF YOU MEAN THE WOMAN WHO CAME TO OUR HOUSE...
HE *IS* MRS. DRUTHERS!

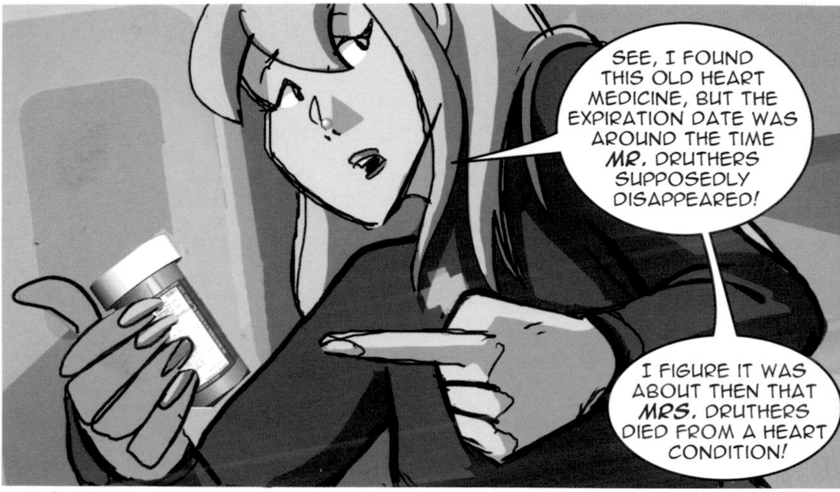
SEE, I FOUND THIS OLD HEART MEDICINE, BUT THE EXPIRATION DATE WAS AROUND THE TIME MR. DRUTHERS SUPPOSEDLY DISAPPEARED!
I FIGURE IT WAS ABOUT THEN THAT MRS. DRUTHERS DIED FROM A HEART CONDITION!

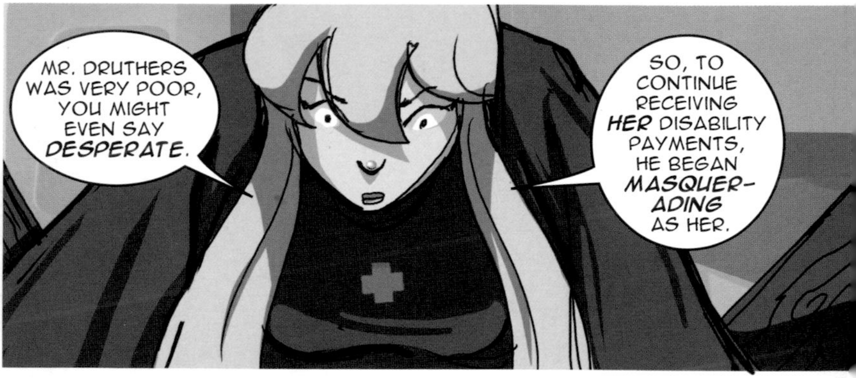
MR. DRUTHERS WAS VERY POOR, YOU MIGHT EVEN SAY DESPERATE.
SO, TO CONTINUE RECEIVING HER DISABILITY PAYMENTS, HE BEGAN MASQUER-ADING AS HER.

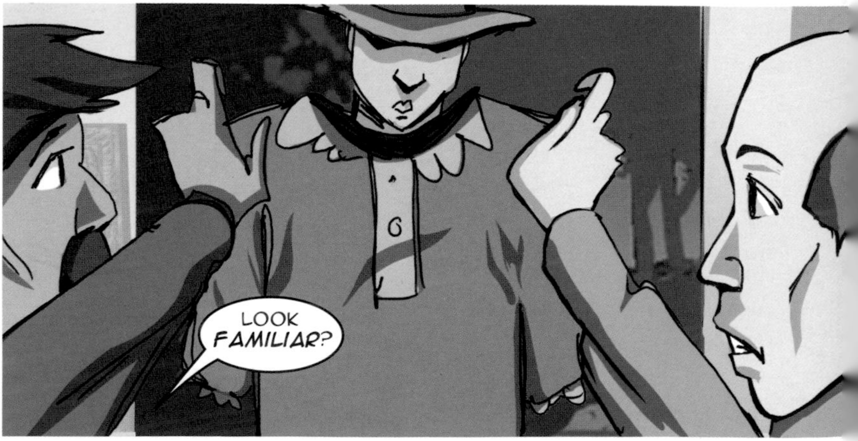
LOOK FAMILIAR?

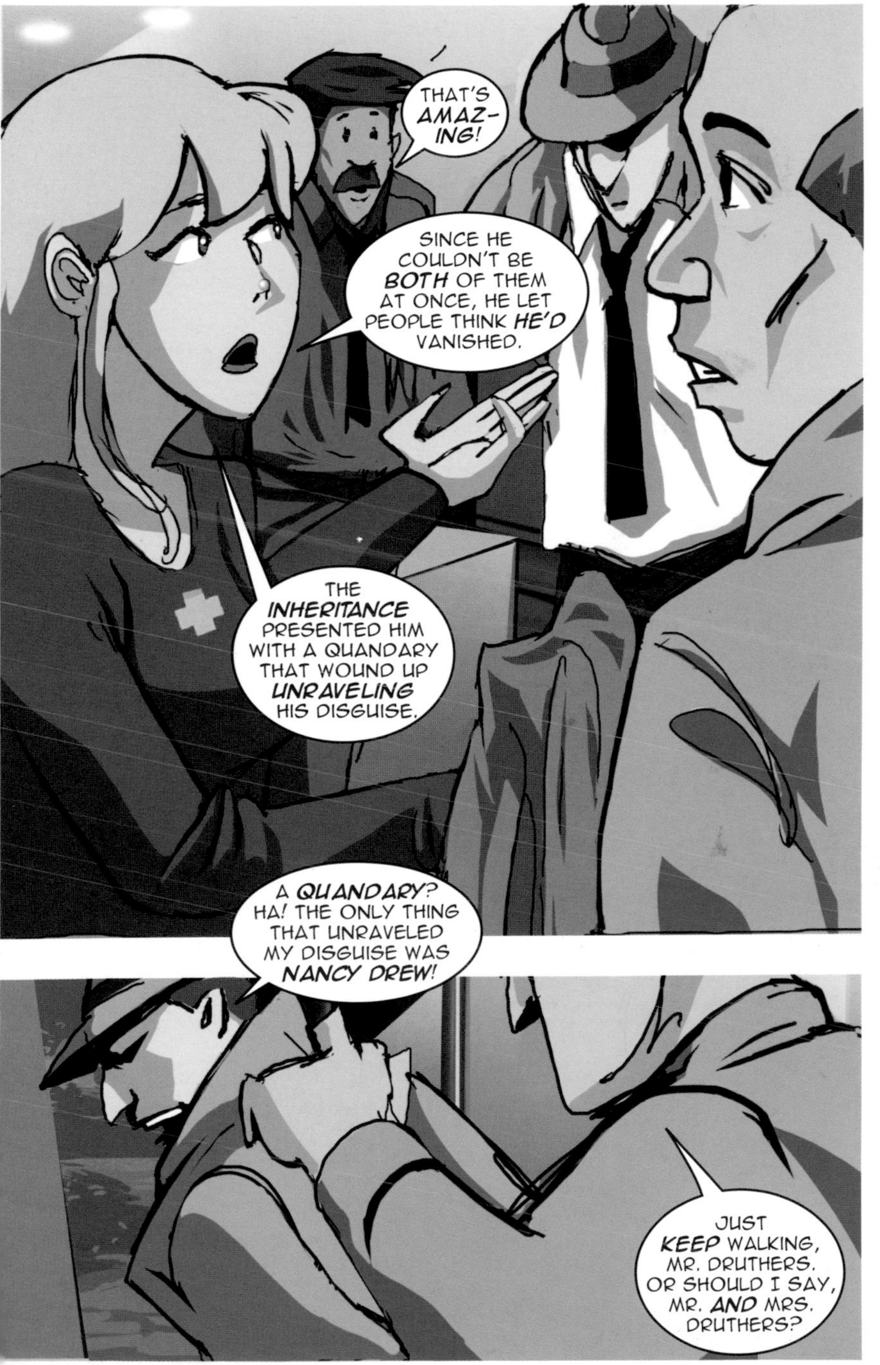
THAT'S AMAZ-ING!
SINCE HE COULDN'T BE BOTH OF THEM AT ONCE, HE LET PEOPLE THINK HE'D VANISHED.
THE INHERITANCE PRESENTED HIM WITH A QUANDARY THAT WOUND UP UNRAVELING HIS DISGUISE.
A QUANDARY? HA! THE ONLY THING THAT UNRAVELED MY DISGUISE WAS NANCY DREW!
JUST KEEP WALKING, MR. DRUTHERS. OR SHOULD I SAY, MR. AND MRS. DRUTHERS?

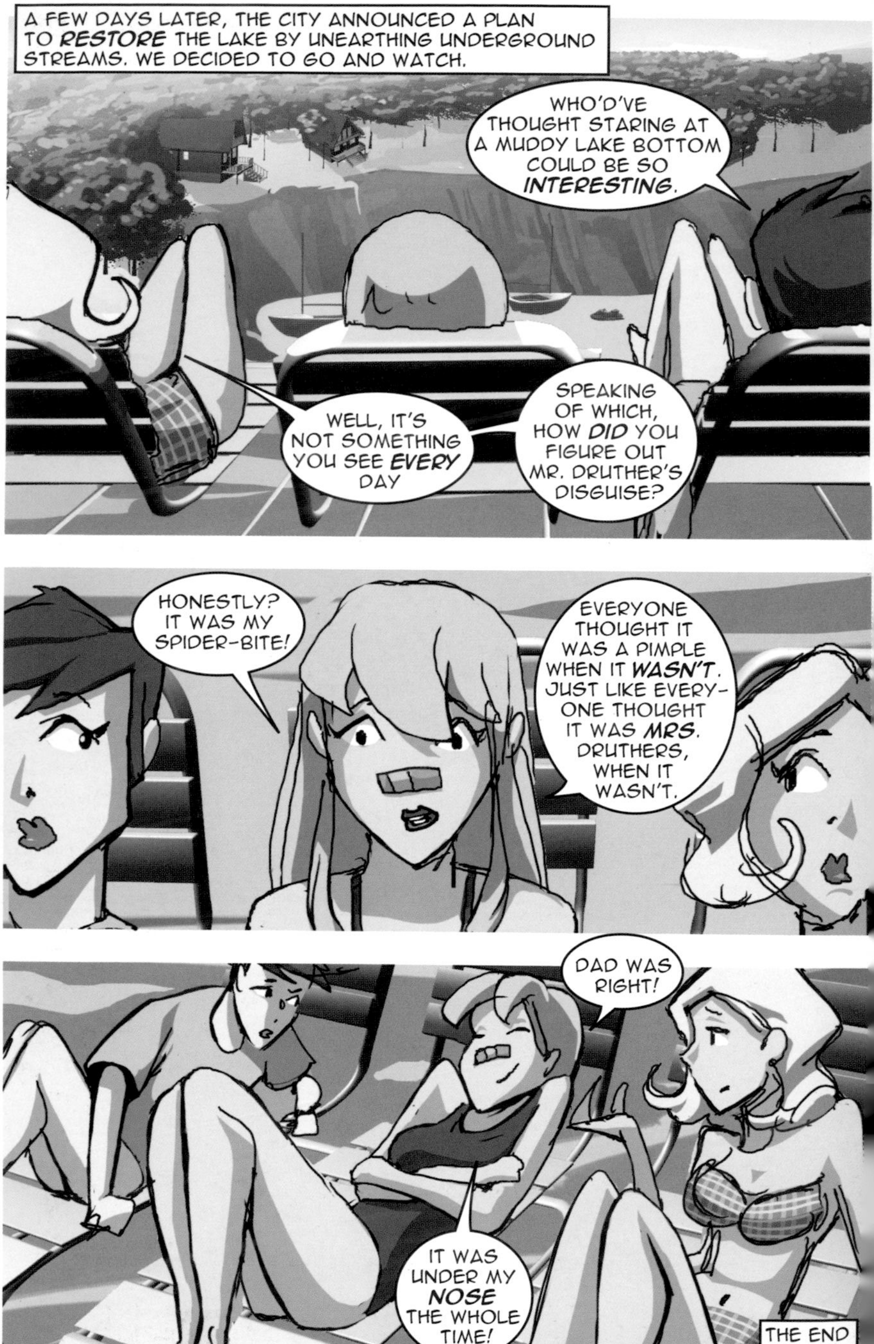
A FEW DAYS LATER, THE CITY ANNOUNCED A PLAN TO RESTORE THE LAKE BY UNEARTHING UNDERGROUND STREAMS. WE DECIDED TO GO AND WATCH.
WHO'D'VE THOUGHT STARING AT A MUDDY LAKE BOTTOM COULD BE SO INTERESTING.
WELL, IT'S NOT SOMETHING YOU SEE EVERY DAY
SPEAKING OF WHICH, HOW DID YOU FIGURE OUT MR. DRUTHER'S DISGUISE?
HONESTLY? IT WAS MY SPIDER-BITE!
EVERYONE THOUGHT IT WAS A PIMPLE WHEN IT WASN'T. JUST LIKE EVERY-ONE THOUGHT IT WAS MRS. DRUTHERS, WHEN IT WASN'T.
DAD WAS RIGHT!
IT WAS UNDER MY NOSE THE WHOLE TIME!
THE END

Special Advance Preview of NANCY DREW Graphic Novel #6 – "Mr. Cheeters Is Missing"

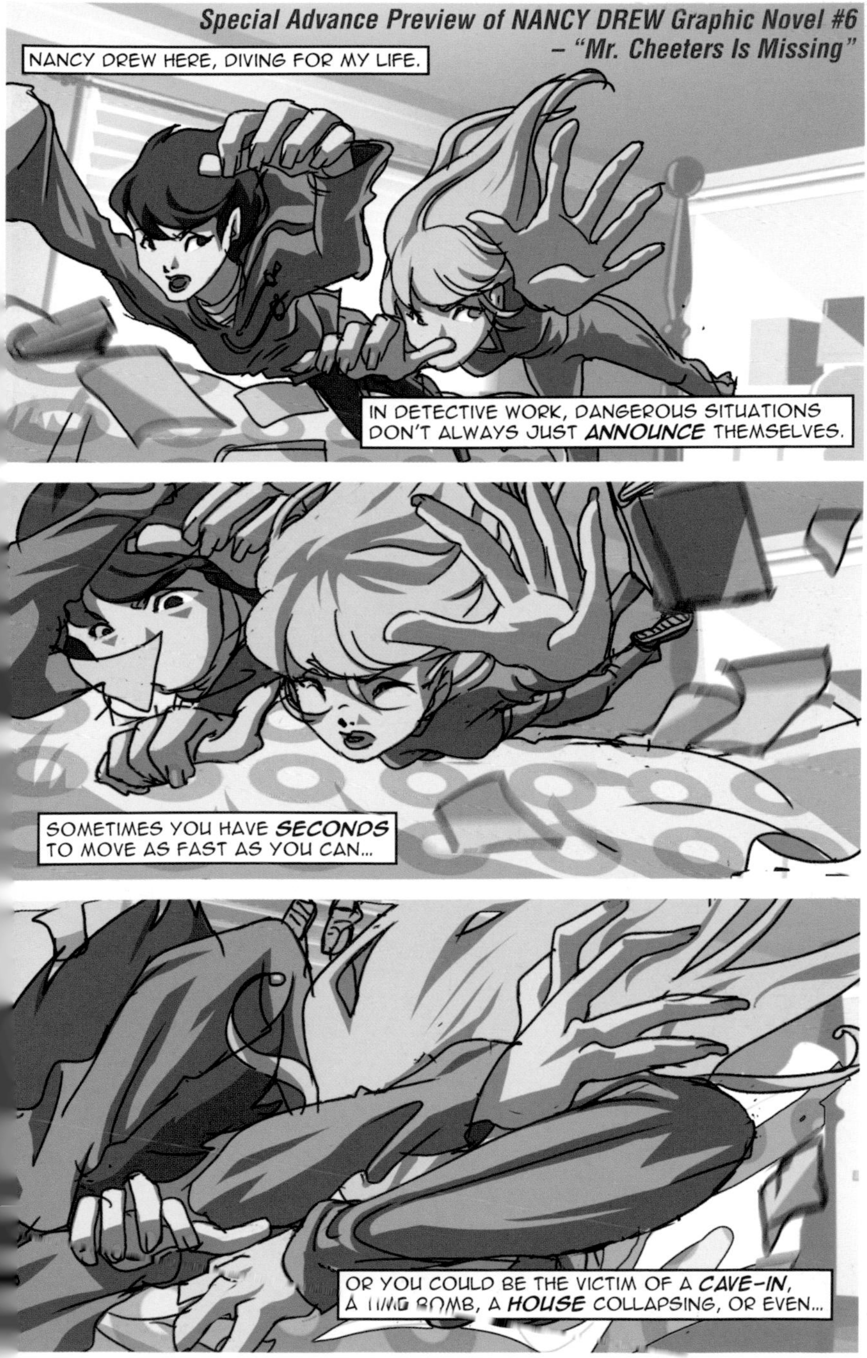
NANCY DREW HERE, DIVING FOR MY LIFE.
IN DETECTIVE WORK, DANGEROUS SITUATIONS DON'T ALWAYS JUST ANNOUNCE THEMSELVES.
SOMETIMES YOU HAVE SECONDS TO MOVE AS FAST AS YOU CAN...
OR YOU COULD BE THE VICTIM OF A CAVE-IN, A TIME BOMB, A HOUSE COLLAPSING, OR EVEN...

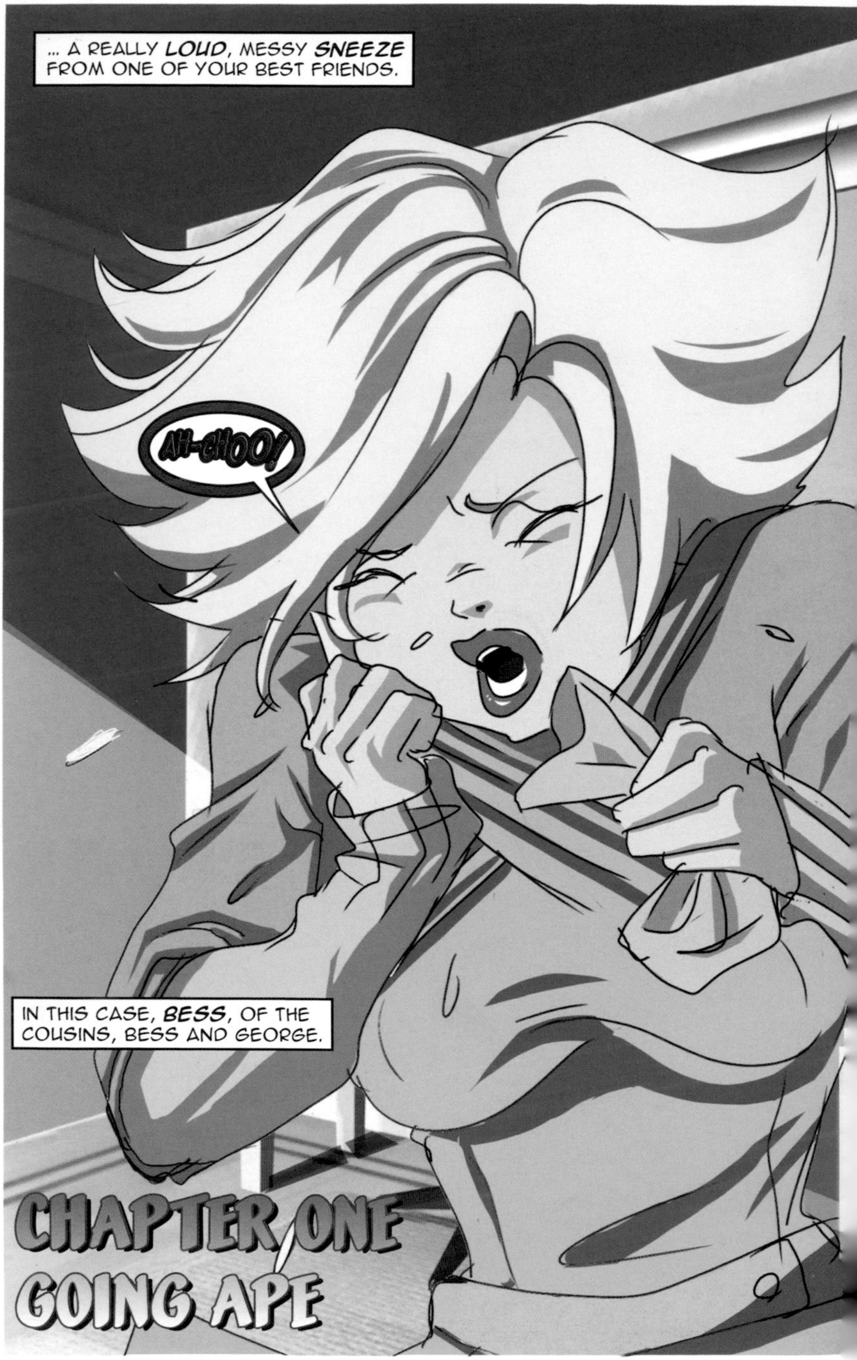
... A REALLY LOUD, MESSY SNEEZE FROM ONE OF YOUR BEST FRIENDS.
AH-CHOO!
IN THIS CASE, BESS, OF THE COUSINS, BESS AND GEORGE.
CHAPTER ONE
GOING APE

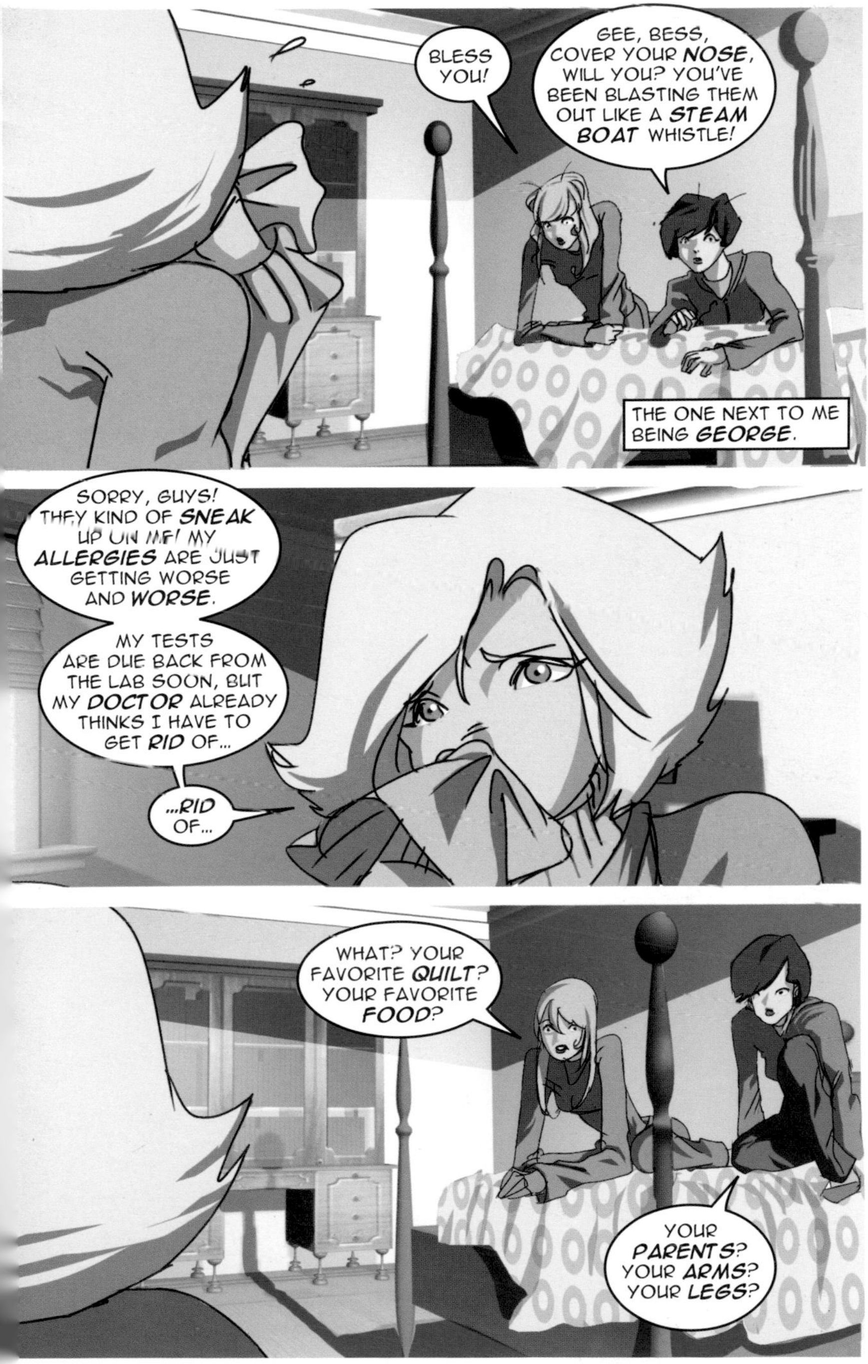
BLESS YOU!
GEE, BESS, COVER YOUR NOSE, WILL YOU? YOU'VE BEEN BLASTING THEM OUT LIKE A STEAM BOAT WHISTLE!
THE ONE NEXT TO ME BEING GEORGE.
SORRY, GUYS! THEY KIND OF SNEAK UP ON ME! MY ALLERGIES ARE JUST GETTING WORSE AND WORSE.
MY TESTS ARE DUE BACK FROM THE LAB SOON, BUT MY DOCTOR ALREADY THINKS I HAVE TO GET RID OF...
...RID OF...
WHAT? YOUR FAVORITE QUILT? YOUR FAVORITE FOOD?
YOUR PARENTS? YOUR ARMS? YOUR LEGS?

Don't miss NANCY DREW Graphic Novel # 6 — "Mr. Cheeters Is Missing"

THE HARDY BOYS

A NEW GRAPHIC NOVEL EVERY 3 MONTHS!

#1 "The Ocean of Osyria", ISBN 1-59707-001-7
#2 "Identity Theft," ISBN 1-59707-003-3
#3 "Mad House," ISBN 1-59707-010-6
#4 "Malled," ISBN 1-59707-014-9
NEW! #5 "Sea You, Sea Me!"
Frank and Joe go undercover aboard the Silver Lining to discover why teenagers have been mysteriously missing.
ISBN 1-59707-022-X
Each: 5x7 1/2, 96pp., full color paperback: $7.95
Also available in hardcover!
$12.95 each.
Vol. 1: ISBN 1-59707-005-X
Vol. 2: ISBN 1-59707-007-6
Vol. 3: ISBN 1-59707-011-4
Vol. 4: ISBN 1-59707-015-7
Vol. 5: ISBN 1-59707-023-8

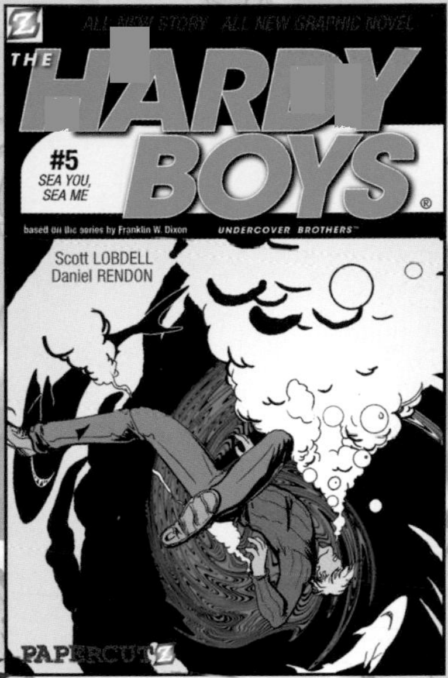

ALL NEW STORY ALL NEW GRAPHIC NOVEL
THE HARDY BOYS®
#5
SEA YOU, SEA ME
based on the series by Franklin W. Dixon
UNDERCOVER BROTHERS™
Scott LOBDELL
Daniel RENDON
PAPERCUTZ

ON SALE NOW!

ZORRO®

#1 "Scars!," ISBN 1-59707-016-5
#2 "Drownings!," ISBN 1-59707-018-1
NEW! #3 "Vultures"
Will Zorro become Vulture-brunch? Could happen when Zorro and Eulalia Bandini encounter Lockspur and J-Man who are bilking artists' widows of thier fortunes.
ISBN 1-59707-020-3
Each: 5x7 1/2, 96pp., full color paperback: $7.95
Also available in hardcover!
$12.95 each.
Vol. 1: ISBN 1-59707-017-3
Vol. 2: ISBN 1-59707-019-X
Vol. 3: ISBN 1-59707-021-1

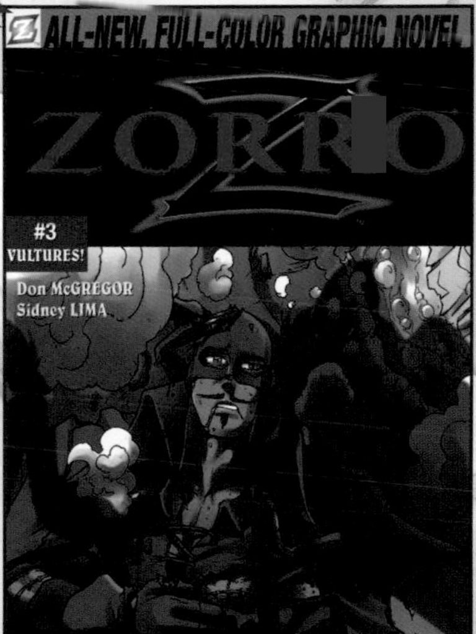

ALL-NEW, FULL-COLOR GRAPHIC NOVEL
ZORRO
#3
VULTURES!
Don McGREGOR
Sidney LIMA
PAPERCUTZ

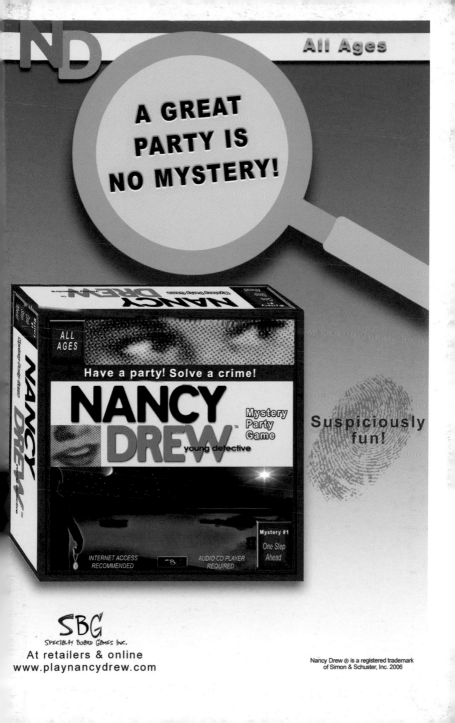